The Man Who Went Away

THE MAN
WHO WENT AWAY

a novel by
THEMISTOCLES HOETIS

PELLEGRINI & CUDAHY   NEW YORK

To Pip and Albert

CONTENTS

৺ 1. AKIN ARAHK

Characters

Akin Arahk   *an oboist*

Alex   *student*

Sir David Dove   *British visitor*

Dorothea   *Sir David's eldest sister*

Letters

To Akin   (from Alex)   *Aboard ship*
Bordeaux
Corsica
Granada
Fez
Upper Nile
Alexandria
To Alex   (from Akin)   *the 31st*

The Morning of the Thirty-first

A hazel-colored Hathor, miniature size, stands on a circular table. The table and an iron-post bed are the furnishings of a rented room in Roselle, New Jersey. And the Hathor is a statue —*the Goddess of Social Joy*—sent to Akin Arahk from the upper Nile by Alex L——, who is now somewhere on the Black Sea. Akin walks to the table, takes the Hathor and holds it for a moment; then she smashes it on the tiled floor below the wash basin. She is angry with Alex for having left her behind.

Akin is going to sit for an hour at the open window, playing an oboe. She sits stiffly, with her chin raised high. Her slender fingers hold the instrument with delicate patronage, while the fragile, reed mouthpiece is brought forward, upward, and is held in mid-air. Her head remains fixed as her eyes search the floor at her feet, where lay two fragments of the broken Hathor. Sharp corners of the mutilated statue project tiny, ragged edges of light across white tiles of the polished flooring.

Akin considers this and closes her eyes. Then her full lips part. As the woodwind is brought nearer, her tongue reaches to receive the dry, elastic blade.

Presently, a thin, plaintive tone begins the first measure.

A high-collared blouse cut from a man's blue and white shirt tightly encircles her soft, elegant neck. From her hips, a flannel skirt falls in neat folds down over her legs. Her long, black hair is combed back to a bundle which gathers just above her collar.

4

A second, penetrating note is played.

Akin leans backward slowly, leisurely crosses her knees. And thus, her refined, proportioned profile is cast sharply into silhouette at the open window. She seems suspended . . . until her body relaxes, then again becomes immobile, framed at the window. Akin plays more lightly now, smoothly; while out of doors, above the mist, broken clouds shield light from an upper, brilliant sky.

As Akin plays, she thinks; first thoughts focused on the vivid image of a postage stamp. She visualizes its oblong shape with a quarter-moon design at the center. Three small stars form a triangle in the dark-green hollow of the partial sphere. Along the upper-left side of the stamp these words are written: *Egypte, Postes, 32 Mills;* and at the opposite side the same words are repeated in intricate, Arabic characters. The stamp is on a cheap envelope. And the envelope was mailed from a port on the Nile.

This is the last letter Akin has received from

5

Alex, sent nine days past. And it is typewritten on sheets of light-weight paper.

One, two, one, two, one. One, two, one, two, one. The composition Akin plays is her own.

At each pause in the rhythm, images of Alex's face appear, disappear, and reappear successively. At length the rhythm establishes a continuous, sustaining flow of pulse and pause, on which an image of Alex's face becomes fixed, unwavering, and clear before Akin's inner eye. It is an oval, olive face with heavy, dark brows and short, brown hair brushed flat against his skull. His eyes appear to have a demanding, intense expression, and they are half hidden behind long, black lashes.

Alex is a first-generation American, born of immigrant parents whose native homes had been sacked by Bulgarian warriors.

One, two, one, two, one. One, two, one, two, one. Once more the music recalls Akin's attention. Alex's face recedes, blurs, and disappears. Akin now concentrates on her playing.

Sometime in the past:

The music is an ode entitled *The Dwelling of the Gods*. It has been composed for Alex as a gift. Akin has written the score at her brother's apartment, where she is now living. She has been living there for the past six months. And she had moved in one week before she met Alex.

And Alex is a student. He has come to the big city from a small town upstate. He has come to continue his studies in medicine. An unexplainable impulse has driven him forever away from his home, his family, and his childhood environment.

During Alex's first days in the city, he is befriended by a relative who is a painter. His relative, a distant cousin, soon introduces Alex to various groups of his student friends. And through these minglings he meets Akin Arahk, an oboist. Although a warm friendship develops between them, neither is willing to commit the other to a bondship, for as yet each of

7

them is uncertain of the sentiment felt toward the other. Even so, they are together frequently.

And nevertheless, on Easter Sunday, Alex announces to Akin that he is leaving the city. He is going to Arizona. His health is bad, he gives as his reason.

The afternoon before the morning of Alex's departure he visits Akin to say goodbye. Akin presents him with her composition.

"The ode is an anniversary gift," explains Akin, holding the manuscript open and watching the expression on Alex's face. "I wrote it in commemoration of the six months we have known each other."

"Bless you, my dear Akin," says Alex in a serious voice to suit the occasion. He gently caresses Akin's forehead with his cheek and stands next to her for a moment. He wishes, to himself, that he had brought along something for her, something beautiful. Then he steps back, as he takes the sheets of music in his hands and begins to inspect them closely.

8

The composition is written in F minor. The notes, rests, sharps and flats are meticulously penned in with India black ink. At the top, left-hand corner of the second page, a curious drawing has been sketched in lightly with pencil—of a man standing erect and wearing a mask made to resemble a cow's head. And on the last page a notation reads: *The Pause placed over the double bar denotes the conclusion of the piece.* With care, Alex continues to look over the finely printed manuscript, until finally he holds the large, folded sheets out at arm's length and turns them one way, then another; and then upside down.

"But in which house does one find these mysterious gods?" he asks whimsically.

Akin, startled, darts back her head. She thinks about the question for a moment before she understands that Alex is joking with her. Then she places her hands superciliously on her hips and begins walking with exaggerated complacency around her brother's expensively decorated drawing-room. "Well, young man,

9

let me tell you," she says, mimicking the mockery of streetwalkers she has seen or has read about. "It's like this . . ."

Alex laughs aloud, catches Akin by the arm, and pulls her over to the couch. "Listen, young lady," says he still laughing, but at the same time forcing Akin to lie beside him, "if you will tell me in what house the gods live, I'll promise to tell you of a strange and interesting dream I had last night."

But Alex's words have frightened Akin somewhat. She hadn't expected this interest in her composition's title which, after all, was only a title. His interest she feels to be insistent; and it frightens her, as if she had played a strange note that sympathetically resounded with unexpected vibrations in the room. Her thoughts are revealed unconsciously in her almond-shaped eyes.

"You see?" he says, "I, too, have a secret."

Akin turns toward Alex, considers him attentively for a moment, hesitates, and then begins. "All right," she remarks closing her eyes, "since you insist on knowing about the gods, I'll tell you."

Akin's Story

"It seems that once upon a time, a great long time ago when the years of civilizations were still numbered by dynasties, there were living together seven gods who dwelt in the House of Horus beside the river Nile."

Akin relaxes beside Alex and speaks slowly, as she proceeds to invent a story adapted to the music she has written for him. "These gods, the story tells us, were gifted with great powers and with knowledge of many secrets that might be called 'magical'; although amongst men of their own time the seven were known only as scholars and as wise men—doctors of philosophy, we might say. In any case, their renown as profound scholars drew to their temple a number of students from all over Egypt and the lands beyond, young neophytes to whom they considered themselves obligated in the duty of presiding over rites of initiation that in those days marked the advance of a student.

"As it was considered most important that

none have access to knowledge of power before
a long discipline of preparation, the seven gods
were vowed, amongst themselves, to reveal their
knowledge to none but to those disciples of
whose capacities and trustworthiness they were
certain. And, therefore, taking the post in rota-
tion day by day, one of the gods was appointed
guard and protector of the rest. For this task, he
who was chosen was obliged to disguise himself
in strange robe and queer headgear as the com-
mon guard of his day. Clothed in this attire, he
stationed himself at the entrance to the House
of Horus."

Here Akin stops.

"Is that all?" inquires Alex, who finds himself peculiarly interested in this peculiar tale.
As yet he has not heard enough.

"No, that isn't quite all," replies Akin, who
pauses before she continues. "It so happened,
as the story goes, that past this particular gate
an exceptionally lovely young woman began to
pass daily, going to and returning from a fresh
spring-well located in a near-by grove of tall,
rich palms. Every morning she passed twice by
this gate, and every seventh morning, from be-

hind his mask, one of the unknown guardians of the seven gods regarded her graceful carriage as she passed, attracted to her fine figure—in which elegance, refinement and simplicity combined to produce a remarkable subtlety of color and of line. Her dress was of finest green linen, although entirely plain. Her few pieces of jewelry were of the simplest sort, but of most elegant workmanship. Her manner was unprepossessing, and yet, at once, assured. She was the loveliest of that type we would call 'Egyptian.'

"Well, as I suppose you already will have guessed, it was only a matter of time for an admiring god's admiration to grow into love, his love to desire. . . . For we know that in those days even the gods, even the mightiest and the most divine, were not beyond human desire."

"Yes," Alex adds quietly, "coming down to us from those times are the stories from every land, of men reaching toward divinity and of the gods descending to desires of flesh."

"According to this old story," continues Akin, "this god, finally, became entirely possessed by his desire for this woman. When she

13

passed by his post on her way to and from the
well, his interest soon became so unmistakably
evident that it wasn't long before the affair between them developed more intimately into
secret meetings, in the manner of lovers outside
of the law—for, you see, the fallen god, all unaware, was lost to this woman; while she, in
turn, was generous to him."

Akin cups one hand and brings it to her
mouth as she coughs lightly. Alex smiles, while
she considers how the story goes on from there.

"You see," Akin remarks, returning to her
story, "this would seem to be a harmless affair
between the god and his beloved—except for
the fact that even a god, in love, in time becomes at a loss to know what he can bestow. At
first he gave her trinkets and jewelry and fine
cloth, then secrets to preserve her beauty; but
finally, such is the nature of divinity, when
these gifts seemed insufficient to him, for his
love's sake, as he thought, he felt compelled to
give her even more. . . . Whereupon, without considering the heavy obligations to his
own circle, one by one he commenced to reveal
the secrets of Horus. He taught her the laws of

14

the earth, the laws of the seasons, as well as his secrets of divination; coming at last to the deeper laws of creation.

"Now, if he had stopped here, all might have remained well. But, of course, he could not stop, for she proved a curious pupil and, besides, he loved her. It wasn't long, therefore, before he had taught her not only the laws of life but a large part of the laws of the destruction of life as well . . . including, such was his blindness, the method, a compound, by which not only men but the gods themselves might be frozen in sleep to the end of time."

"What an absurd story!" Alex exclaims; he has, nevertheless, been listening attentively to Akin's recital. "I suppose she puts everyone in the House of Horus to sleep in the end?" He smiles cynically, for Alex feels he must make note of the absurdity in Akin's tale, when in fact his interruption springs from a need to take hold of himself. He feels the strange, frightening sensation of a person who finds himself living in the dream of his unconscious childhood, a dream that, as an unthinking youngster, had made his blood run cold and for weeks thereafter had filled his nights with fear and anxiety.

Now he insists to Akin, who has not spoken since his interruption, "Tell me, then, does she put everyone to sleep?" His voice lifts, "and even the god who loved her?"

Akin meanwhile has opened her eyes and is wondering what to make of her own story. Alex has provoked her. This isn't the first time his interruptions have leapt before her to a conclusion, and now she searches for a new ending. They lie quietly side by side until she speaks again.

"No, the woman doesn't put the god to sleep, although you are right in having guessed her intention. In this story the woman, the would-be betrayer of this god, is betrayed by one of her own people. How this happened, the story doesn't tell us. We only know that the god was informed of her intentions in time to prevent her act against the gods—whereupon, from a divinity in love, giving all, he became in turn a divinity in revenge, merciless, transforming her into a mammoth statue, and the

16

statue was placed opposite him at the gate where he stood guard. And there she stands yet, from that long, far-off time until this day, a remembrance and a warning at the entrance to the dwelling of the gods." Akin concludes her final remarks and smiles openly in triumph.

"But she was a silly girl," Alex breaks in, as he laughs at his own earlier fears from the events of this tale. "She trumps everything in the end." He stops for a moment. He is searching for an ending to surpass Akin's own. Then he adds, "That's what she gets for having her own human lover while making up to the god."

"I guess you're right," agrees Akin. He has managed to detect the true climax after all, thinks she; and now her lovely ending sounds weak. "Anyway, all women are silly in the end. But now you must tell me that very interesting dream you had," she adds, smiling and repeating his challenge.

"My dream is far more real than your story of the gods who dwell in the House of Horus, I'm afraid," Alex remarks in a provocative tone of voice. "You will see." He is annoyed with

17

himself for having made such a drama of Akin's story. And meanwhile he clears his thoughts to organize the dream in his mind; then he repeats, "It's a good dream, you'll see. It's about you and me."

"Will you allow interruptions or comments?" asks Akin sharply, in order to place emphasis on Alex's previous rudeness.

"No, of course not. The dream must be told straight. If it isn't, I'll become confused and the meaning will be lost." Then Alex unexpectedly feels quite guilty for his lack of diplomacy a moment ago. "Is that all right with you?"

"Yes, of course," Akin says, laughing easily and closing her eyes once more.

A few minutes later:

Alex's Dream

"Well, in the first place, I had already returned from Arizona, from my health cure. I had finished my studies, but my degree was given to me torn in shreds. This isn't especially important in the dream, yet I mention it because I want to keep all the sequences in order. Every small detail counts. Well then, at the start you and I were standing near an open window, in a room I had never known before, in a house located in a small town outside of a large city. It was autumn, and for no apparent reason there we were, standing at an open window, talking about our destinies. It was you who spoke first. You said, 'Now that your hair has grown long, Alex, let's promise never to separate again.' That was a curious statement you made, I thought to myself; nevertheless, when I took hold of my hair I discovered that it had grown long enough to rest on my shoulders. Whereupon I turned to you and said, 'I believe you are quite correct. It's odd, wouldn't you say? that the condition of my health should be revealed in such an obvious symbol. Hair—isn't that crazy?' I ran my fingers through my hair, which seemed to be growing longer even there before your eyes. I then said, 'As I think of it, I was just about to suggest the same thing: about promising never to separate. But I believe you knew what was on my mind all along. You saw it because my hair had grown long!' Then you smiled at me as though I were a foolish child, and I pretended not to notice."

Alex pauses, rubs his hands several times, then says, "A thought occurred to me right at that instant, and so I said, 'In fact, on the train coming back I decided that we should leave America.' You smiled again, you smiled as though you had known these thoughts also. 'This country is not for us, Akin. We don't belong here. Let's leave it. Let's go far away.' You only smiled. I said, 'Let's go to Europe. Let's go to France. America won't allow us the liberty, the individuality, to continue doing the things we desire. I've learned all these things in the army,' I said to you. 'America will never erect statues for people like us; I've learnt all this in the army,' I repeated. Now, I cannot explain why I should speak to you like that—about leaving together, things about America, and especially about the army! And in a dream! As I think about it now, I don't remember ever having spoken to you about being in the army. And yet, you see, I *was* in the army, funny thing, in the medical corps. However, let me go on with the facts of the dream. . . .

"I looked over the small village which lay outside the window. Beyond the stretch of little houses I could see low hills that rose and fell to the edge of a wide river, a river lined with tracks and docks and boats of all descriptions. There were trains being loaded and unloaded at sidings, boats loading and unloading at the docks, large cranes swinging back and forth at work in the transfer of cargo. Everywhere, activity and business. I looked further along in that strange perspective of a dream, past drying nets of fishermen in from the sea, and there were crowds of old people, all sitting on great, long yellow benches in the sun. They were amusing themselves on the commotion and energy of the port. I was no longer at the window, but in the middle of it all. I walked along behind the line of benches and spotted my mother. I didn't speak to her, however,—when then, unexpectedly, I spoke to you, for you were standing next to me.

"Just at that moment, as we were starting to

21

talk, my mother turned around and faced me. 'Darling, there you are,' she said. 'I'm so glad you're home, home for good. Take a little rest and then find yourself a nice, steady job, something that you would like, a job with the city hospital; that would be nice. That's a good boy. And if you find the right girl—she must be bright and not too pretty—you can save your money and marry one day,' she said. And not taking notice that someone was standing there beside me.

"I turned to you, for we were back at the open window by now, and I said, 'Don't you see, Akin? That's exactly what I don't want to do. I don't want to get a job, marry, settle down.'

At that point you smiled at me, sympathetically this time, and you nodded your head in agreement with my complaint. I then said, 'No, Akin, now that I am back, healthy, and with a broader perspective on things, we must leave at once. Let's say goodbye to all the nonsense,' said I, and then I awoke."

"It is certainly a queer dream," says Akin, raising herself from the couch and walking over to the wash basin. "Do you suppose it's a premonition?"

"How should I know? It may easily be that, if you're a superstitious person." Alex laughs quietly and walks over to Akin. "Wouldn't it be strange if the dream came to pass? If when I return from Arizona you are living in a room outside of town. . . . And we stand at a window talking about our destinies and about leaving for Europe together?"

Akin is nearing the end of her composition. Alex's face reappears in the pauses of the music. She speaks out to him in her thoughts. "When you came back, did we go away, Alex? Did we say goodbye to all the nonsense?"

The contours of Alex's face are now clear before her.

"No! Alex. You went home—back to your sister, back to your brother-in-law, back to your mother! And how many times did I see you when you got back? Answer me! Alex. How many times?"

Akin places the oboe on her lap. She looks over the roof-tops—flat outcroppings like so many slabs of mud and rock. The roof-tops were like mud and rock then, also, thinks Akin to herself. And as she looks down to the street below, she sees again how it was then. Alex is approaching the rooming house, waving to her excitedly, as he had done then:

"Akin! Akin! It's me! Alex!"

"Alex! Alex! Is it you? It's you! You're back!" screams Akin from her window and waves both arms out at him. "Wait! Wait until I come down and unlock the front door!"

She hurries down the three flights of stairs, but upon reaching the door, she is unable to open it.

"Turn the key on your side," she says to Alex in a loud voice through the door. "It's locked from the outside."

"There's no key on *this* side," shouts he laughingly. He pushes the door several times with his shoulder, as though threatening to break it down. "Guess I'll have to go away again," he says. "Don't see why I ever came all the way over to this god-forsaken town, just to

24

find the door locked. Guess I'll have to go away," he repeats and pretends to descend the outside stair by stamping on the wooden landing.

"Alex! Alex! Don't go!" Akin screams as she turns the knob back and forth in exasperation. "Wait Alex! Wait until I get the key from the landlady," she says. "Alas!" And runs off to the back of the house, off through the long corridor.

Alex has been back from Arizona since the summer began. From his cousin he has learned that Akin moved from her brother's apartment. He has been told that she lives in a rooming house on Eighth Street in Roselle, New Jersey. Yet he has made no effort to reach her, to see her, until now.

"Didn't your cousin give you my address?" asks Akin, after unlocking the door and leading Alex to her room.

He doesn't reply. Akin walks to one corner of the room and begins preparing coffee in an electric pot set on the floor. "I gave him the number two days before leaving my brother's

25

place. He promised me that he would let you know the moment you returned."

"I didn't see my cousin, Akin," Alex says. "I didn't see anyone. I can't explain. But when I got back I didn't want to see anyone." He sits down. "I couldn't." He is seated on the edge of the bed with his hands to his face. "I can't tell you why, Akin. I barely know why myself. That's the way it was, nevertheless. I didn't want to see anyone." There is a short silence between them.

"Never mind, Alex," says Akin, looking at him from a kneeling position across the room. "Don't tell me if you're not certain about it. Whatever you did, you did. That's reason enough." Akin lifts the cover off the electric pot and steam, fresh coffee steam, fills the room. "So don't think about it at all. It was probably the right thing to do anyway." She arranges her two cups.

"But I do want to think about it, Akin," says he suddenly. He slowly draws his hands away from his face and places them on his knees. "I should never have gone back to my family. It was a mistake."

"The coffee is ready, Alex." She looks up once more and adds in a soft voice, "Perhaps we should talk about it later."

During the nine months Alex was away, his health became even worse. Periodic headaches developed which interfered with and distracted him away from his studies. He began frequenting bars and night clubs. He drank in great quantities, from an uncertain desire to free himself of this mysterious malady. The doctor at the university hospital advised him to return East, to go home. He became one of those 'case histories' who persist in a routine long after it has become drained of sense. He arrived at class defiant or drunk. On two occasions he had fits of uncontrollable anger when he stormed to the head of his music class to beat the keys of the piano with his fists, while cursing his instructor with vile language.

"Things ran smoothly for me in Arizona. The university was a snap," says Alex, after finishing his coffee and stretching himself across the bed. He makes a pillow by crossing his arms behind his head, letting one leg slide to the floor. Alex is relaxed, but he speaks to Akin with what is to her an unaccustomed emptiness in his voice. "Everything progressed ordinarily until spring. Then the school semester was over and I found myself with nothing special to do for the summer. For some reason the idea of seeing California struck my fancy. I don't know why. But I wrote my family for money. In reply they sent a ticket—a ticket back home. I tried to get a refund on that, but there was nothing doing. At that point there was nothing I could do, Akin, nothing but to return. You can see the predicament I was in." He is silent, watching Akin across the room.

Akin takes the cups to the wash basin, returns to the bed and sits next to Alex. "You should have written to one of us, Alex. We would have raised the money, had you let us know what was happening."

"I should have written. I know that now, Akin." He covers his face once more.

"I missed you, Alex," says Akin just then, as though revealing a deep secret which no one

28

was to know. A tear rolls down over Akin's high cheek bone.

"I missed you, also, Akin," says he. Alex raises himself from his stretched position and sits next to her on the side of the bed. "There were many times when I thought of you and wished that you were with me. You know. I tried a dozen times to get one of the regular music students to play the ode you had written for me. And everytime I'd finally arrange a date or an appointment, something would turn up. The student didn't arrive. I couldn't get away from class. The instrument was locked away. Invariably something would come up, and I never got to hear it even once." Alex stands up and begins walking to the window. His hands are in his pockets. He turns to Akin in his old, laughing manner. "Do you know what I did at last? I had the manuscript framed. I hung it over the desk in my room." Alex feels uneasy. He looks at Akin; then goes to the window. He is afraid to face the girl in the room "Akin?" says he, almost to himself.

"Yes, Alex?" she replies, folding her hands on her lap. She has the feeling that there is

something he has not told her, something
which she should know.

"I'll never again go back to my family,
Akin," he adds abruptly. He folds his arms.
"I'm fed up. That's it. Fed up with myself. Fed
up with my family, with schools, with washing
dishes for my brother-in-law!" He turns around
and traces the line of his shadow on the floor.
"Once we talked—about leaving together."

"Yes, Alex," says she. "I missed you, Alex,"
Akin says to herself.

"I really want to go. We must go, Akin. This
isn't the place for us, Akin. We don't belong
here. Our sort never will. I'm fed up with the
whole damned country! . . . If I could make
my way, just a little. If the value of our nation
wasn't balanced by the fractional weight of an
atom. If there were any chance of personal liberty, Akin!" He thinks to himself a moment,
looking out the window and over the roof-tops.
Then he turns, "Perhaps it isn't America. Perhaps it is simply that things are bad all over
right now." He pauses again. "It's a crazy world,
Akin. Everywhere you go it's a crazy world. Is
it the same everywhere, Akin? I must know.

But here—the studies, the dishes, the chemicals and cures. My relatives! I despise them all. We must go, Akin. You've got to come with me. I need you." He stops.

"Yes, Alex," Akin speaks softly. She knows that she has spoken these words before. "Let's go away."

Alex walks back to the bed, sits down, and takes Akin's hands. "I shall move down here to Roselle, to your room. And we can begin making plans." He starts to tremble. "The agreement is this: We'll wait." He looks into Akin's eyes as though to make a declaration. "I'll find work before the week is over." His hand moves to her shoulder.

"It's Thursday," says Akin, and with three fingers of one hand she commences to unbutton his blue and white shirt. "You can't get work on Thursday, Alex. Roselle is a slow town. Jobs are impossible to get here. Wait, Alex. Wait until Monday. Go to Manhattan on Monday and see what you can find there."

"Yes, of course. I should have realized that myself. I'll go to Manhattan on Monday and see what I can find there." Alex again stretches

31

himself out on the bed. "I can inquire at the establishments on Forty-Second Street. I can tell them I worked in Poughkeepsie all summer long at my brother-in-law's place. I'll write to Theodore and have him confirm this, should an employer care to speculate. Theodore says they are always short of workers. He says jobs like that are easily found, even in the city." Alex touches Akin's hand lightly. "What difference does it make what I do? It doesn't matter, not really. What we need is food. That's all. Money for food and money for rent. After those problems are taken care of, we can begin saving money for our trip. You'll see, Akin. It will be easy. And I'll tell them, besides, that I've had plenty of experience washing dishes in the army. That's simple."

Two weeks after he has moved to Roselle, Alex is still unable to find work. One morning, without word to Akin, he purchases a third-class ticket to Bordeaux, for himself, with money he has earned the preceding summer by washing dishes. And he is gone.

Akin is looking out into the gray mist. She raises the reed to her lips and commences playing the composition from its beginning.

Alex! You didn't keep your promise! is Akin's next thought. Had you kept to your agreement, had you waited a few weeks, surely I would have gotten the money myself. I could have earned it. I would have borrowed it from a friend. Or if not that, I would have earned it by playing oboe with a small orchestra. One way or another, no matter how, I would have earned my passage to go with you. I am certain, Alex, certain that had you given me time I would have raised the money somehow. And too, Alex, I know that you knew this!

What difference does it make now? says Akin to herself as she nears the first third of her music for the second time. You couldn't wait, Alex. For you were possessed.

Aboard Ship

My dearest Akin:

A queer world! said I, even then. God

threatened to strike us dead whenever we tried to change it.

In those days when my adolescence evoked in me intense irrationalities, I found that my life at home with my mother and my sister had little or no sympathy. In fact, I do admit, I knew well this same disposition even in the days when my father was alive. That my life at the university seemed to me like a constitutional peg in the ground, around which I ran continuous circles, was only too evident. At the time, when I began regarding my desires to leave the family behind, without doubt or, furthermore, question, the course of my action was inevitable. On the sixth day of the new year, I packed what belongings I most dearly treasured, and while the snow fell heavily, I boarded the evening train with my mind headlong. And this, also: I was determined not to look back, never thereafter to return, however difficult and impossible I should find my life before me.

I arrived in the great city and opened my arms. I soon located my distant cousin, who was of my own age and temperament. And it

was because of his moral support and guid-
ance that I gained what footing and meagre
security were obtainable under those strenuous circumstances. I was restless however,—
even when after I had met you, Akin—and
altogether misled by the cosmopolitan society
which I gradually came to loathe. What with
the impressions I sketched in my own mind
concerning the behavior and lack of sincerity
which to me were the obvious traits of my
contemporaries, I lost all faith. In relation to
this, my character and personality developed
firmly. And so to my personality, however
arrogant, and moreover conspicuously anti-
social, I clung savagely.

I did make many restrictions. To be sure,
in due course my companions—those who
were to be my life-long friends (at that time
my cousin, at that time you, at that time, etc.,)
and those 'one-night stands' my attraction for
whom was purely of a physical nature—
dwindled down to less than a handful. One
hungry day it dawned on me that that which
I had been expecting would descend upon
me from either accidental or predetermined

force; it would occur in no matter what city, village, or countryside I should find myself at the time. And for this reason I left for Arizona. My family agreed to assist my education there if I promised to continue with medicine. Nevertheless, I made it known that the reason for my departure was 'health reasons.'

And it was then that I came to see you; I had come to say goodbye. You were very kind to me, Akin. Your gift had made such a strong impression on me that immediately upon arriving at my destination, I put it away and did not touch it once. To me your *Ode* was a divination of some strange sort, for which to release it from its own paper was to lose it forever. And thus I kept it intact, somewhat afraid of its power.

By spring of this past year—in fact, on the day when Easter fell on a Monday—I faced the fact that I was quite lost, incapable, actually, of forming any degree of normal compatability with my race and civilization. The times I found this attitude to exist in me most sharply were when the everyday and the not-so-everyday people about me, and in my class-rooms, seemed little more than a régime of unbearable locusts. I lost self-control and had seizures, of disastrous effect on all concerned. And then I was advised to return home. So I wrote to my family and told them I wanted them to take me back. They did send for me. And I did return.

I did not want you nor the others to see me in this condition, Akin; so I stayed away. I intentionally took what I thought would be a simple job—in contradiction to what my beliefs had been up until then. I washed dishes the entire summer. But this, too, failed miserably.

I wanted to get away once again. You, more than anyone else I knew, would be the only person to understand, I thought then; so I came to you. But things went queer again.

I found myself lying to you, at the same moment feeling that I was in love with you for the first time. I stayed, and we planned. Yet all along, every minute of the two weeks we had together, I knew it was all impossible. You, me, that room, the whole thing. I left,

so that I could have a chance to think it over.
And I have. I have thought about it until
now. I have concluded that I love you, Akin.
I love you and cannot live without knowing
you will someday be with me once more.
With all my deepest affection,

Alex

What did you find impossible Alex? Me?
Yourself? The room? You say. But I cannot understand. I'm inclined to think that there was
some other reason. Some reason which you refuse to speak about.

Akin is still playing; Akin is still thinking.
Perhaps it was the music which distracted you.
Perhaps it frightened you? Was it the strange
awareness of finding yourself back in your
dream? But I do not see how these things could
possibly have troubled you, knowing that you
have always been so logical and so objective
about these matters. And too, had you loved me
Alex, loved me as I loved you, you would not
have phoned me from the dock to say goodbye.

38

Without seeing me. You were ashamed of yourself then, Alex. I know this now.

Bordeaux

You may have thought that my reason for
not wanting you to see me off at my departure was because I was ashamed of myself,
that I felt guilt at having left you behind. I
must explain myself. I assure you, my dearest Akin, that this is not what I felt. My only
conscious motivation for leaving you in the
manner I did, and I cannot attribute it to
any other source, was because I felt that
otherwise it would be difficult for both of us
at that crucial moment. You shall soon see
that I've not made error by my actions. The
moment I can see my path clearly, I shall find
some means for sending passage money to
you. You will then know that my judgement
in parting alone, first, has been best. Meanwhile, I shall write to you every day.

He writes to her every day. This is true.

39

Paris, Chantilly, Beaumont, Chartres, Lyon, Menton, Nice, Cannes, Marseilles. But what good are the letters? Akin reflects as the mouthpiece is brought down from her lips. She faces her chair around, toward the center of the room, and her eyes follow the lines of a pattern made on the opposite wall where plaster has fallen. I am not there, with you, enjoying the splendor of countries and cultures we both had talked about since first we met, she says to herself. And just as well; that which you write me, if the dates and salutations were to be dismissed, I could read in travelogues.

Corsica

Akin:

You reproach me for my past letters to you, letters of my travels, as being the preoccupations I am disposed to, when evading the issues of the heart for want of an easier way out. And I do confess my mention of the bond which exists between us has been not too frequent these past months. However, this is not due to a loss of feeling and of warmth toward you—not at all. In fact, the contrary. I write to you about my travels so that you may share with me those things which for the moment I am obliged to experience alone. Moreover, the letters may prove to be beneficial; for even though I have never possessed facility or exceptional aptitude for serious writing, I have begun correspondence with a publisher in Paris who is interested in a *Journal* written by an American medical student travelling abroad. Of course I have not mentioned the fact that I no longer study medicine, and particularly since I have always been more or less of a failure in scientific studies; yet I feel that the *Journal* may be the means of getting enough money so as to send for you at last.

Then why not return, Alex? continues Akin. She then recounts questions which heretofore have been answered by him. You have had time, time to find a way to send for me. And as for your travels,—I am beginning to wonder what, exactly, it is that you are looking for.

41

Granada

I repeat to you: I cannot return just yet. To return at this point would mean damnation, expulsion from the heavenly voices themselves and damnation to all the discords of Hell. Since I know that the mystical impulse has always intrigued you and has given you an altar whereon you place all your confidences, then I appeal to that instinct in you if another you cannot see.

Ahead of me I see the outline of an oasis which may in advent merely prove to be but another disastrous plunge. But should I be edged to retrace my recently planted tracks, I will lose my course when attempting a second footing. So, you see; *Never Return,* I know. How could I return now that I am gaining ground on the true reason for having departed? The things I see, the people I meet, the directions I have taken are all quite familiar to me in the dark of my mind. I left when I left! And that in itself is conclusive enough. Why return? only to rattle anew. I have been given my beginning once, and for me to threaten destiny now would be to provoke a fatal challenge.

That is not a conclusive reason! If that were true, in this same sense, I could call the time that you left for Arizona a first beginning. These are all the same beginnings. Don't you see that, Alex? What is it that you are running from? If you will only confide in me, perhaps I can be of help.

Fez

I am getting nearer, each day, to the core of that overwhelming force which has been pulling me from the start. The only thing I lack is my not having you here with me.

Do you have what you want, Alex? Is it independence? Is it denial of your own people? Is it denial of your own society and times? What

43

about me, Alex? For I am alone, alone in my painful dilemma.

Upper Nile

My dear Akin:

The other day I spent long hours packing. While trying to manage space in my small trunk for the odds and ends which I happened to bargain best from an insufferable Jewish merchant who followed me around on my first voyage to the Upper Nile, it occurred to me to ask you whether or not you had received the small statue I posted some time back. A Hathor. Actually, I bought the object especially for you, since the inscription found under its feet, translated, reads: "The House of Horus." It was here where dwelt the gods of love. I am anxious to know if the 'goddess' arrived intact, all in one piece.

I leave Egypt in three weeks, by cargo ship which will take me to the Black Sea. To Turkey then. How long I will remain in Turkey only God knows. Perhaps it will be then,

44

there, in Turkey where I will earn the money about which I have so long spoken.

Affectionately,

Alex

P.S. Meanwhile, I have given your address to a charming British couple whom I first met in Paris, then again in Morocco, and just last week here in Egypt. Most likely they will be in America by the time you receive this letter. I do hope you find them amusing—she with her seven poodles, and he with his black umbrella always chasing after them. Sir David Dove, and his sister Dorothea.

"Hello, hello! Are you there?" a high-pitched voice says to Akin the moment the receiver is handed to her by the landlady.

"Hello," says Akin.

"I should like very much to have a word with Miss Akin Arahk, if you please."

"Speaking."

"Oh, there you are! I'm so delighted! I'm calling you on the direction of Mr. Alex L——, whom I met abroad while travelling through

45

Europe and North Africa. My name is David Dove."

"Yes, of course. Alex wrote that you would be visiting the city."

"I'm so delighted that poor Alex let you know in advance of our arrival. I'm here with my eldest sister, Dorothea, and we are frightfully lost in this immense city. . . . Yes, we are quite bewildered by it all. But if you could help orient us a little? You know, an itinerary to last us the duration of our visit. Perhaps you could spare a moment this evening to dine with us?"

"I shall be delighted."

"That's quite decent of you, Miss Arahk. A pleasure for us. And would it inconvenience you frightfully to pick us up here? Difficult, you know, for us foreigners to be wandering about without a guide."

"Naturally."

"That will be most pleasant, then. We're staying at the Park-Madison Towers—a dreadful place, this—but quite manageable to find if one can bear the insolence of a taxi-driver."

"Yes, I'll find it."

46

"At quarter past seven, shall we say?"

"Quarter past seven will be fine."

"Then we'll look for you about that time. Cheerio!"

"Goodbye."

At seven-thirty Akin presses the buzzer at Suite 412. The door opens slowly. Seven poodles dash at her and begin barking and scratching at her heels.

"Myrtle! Bridget! Hilda!" a woman's voice screams from within. "Come to Mommy!"

One, two, one, two, one. One, two, one, two, one. Akin's lips are bleeding from the tight grip her teeth have held on the mouthpiece. The instrument now feels weighted. Her posture has fallen and she begins to feel faint. Alex's face appears once more—his intense eyes; his short, brown hair; the movement of his jaws, as though he is about to speak.

"Alex," speaks out Akin in her thoughts, "the child I bear is yours! Yours, Alex."

She waits a moment. There is no reply.

"You owe it to yourself, Alex, as well as to

47

me, as well as to the child, to return!"

And still no reply.

The oboe falls to the floor. Akin does not move. Her arms are still out, her hands are poised for the keys, her chin is still held high, and the bleeding continues. "The child! The child. The child is yours! Alex."

A silence prevails. Akin's mind wanders back to the letter in the vermilion vase that stands on a shelf in the closet.

Alexandria

I am SHOCKED by the news this morning: I've asked myself, How could this have been and not have been suspected? Not to have been suspected even once! Why? I ask, why had she not spoken of this to me before? A word, a hint, or lie! Months, weeks, days sooner. Insane world! This, our lives.

Incredulous anguish nourished instantly I read your words: "Alex, the child I bear is yours." And even now, this same anguish is with me as I sit here to unfold before you the inertia and despair which have taken hold of my rational mind.

48

To be strung with threads of insensibility like this! My thoughts like monster birds at night dart amongst the planes where lay the ripe dead. I cry to you! My dearest Akin. Listen, me.

Something stands between me and my desires. Beneath my shrouds of logical amour there rests a field, a reservoir of lost, unknown emotions. Call it the heart at the center of things, if you wish. But this heart beating in me—around me, above and below me—me compels. Me, it forces. Me, it compels, beyond my conscious desire to elude time and to bring closer those things which satisfy my lustful heart. And so because of this, because of this instinct, I am obliged to deny existence of responsibility for this child. I feel no responsibility toward the child which still lies sleeping in your womb. I can only offer pleas of remorse to your present sufferings. Listen to me, my beloved Akin. For to misunderstand will be danger to us both.

If there is still time, find a way to remove the seed before it springs to life! Destroy it,

Akin. Destroy it, before it will be too late. For there is nothing in this world but grievance should we bring this child to being. We have nothing to gain. And all is lost. The little we have had, "our own lives," will then be altogether lost in time. You must. Akin, you must bring your contradiction to an end.

This morning, also, I received a cablegram from the publisher in Paris. He has agreed to advance me the sum I have asked for the *Journal*. The money will be waiting for me upon my arrival in Constantinople. Once I have found a suitable place, once you are well enough to travel, I shall send for you.

For we, you and I, must discover within ourselves first, then with the outer world, before the divine hand of creation be given us. So leave it thus for now. Leave it to the winds, or to another. If not forever, at least this time.

Courage!   *Alex*

"Alex! Alex!" screams Akin.
She rises and faces toward the open window.

"Why should you write these things to me? How could you have loved me and have gone without me!" Her voice echoes over the roof tops and falls down, past the low hills, down the industrious river. "Alex, what evil demon has possessed you?"

Should she conclude that what he meant was not love after all? It may be that, she thinks as she sits on the chair once more and takes the oboe in her hands. It may be that: it may be the reason he left his country when he did; the reason he speaks of death now may be that, and not because of financial circumstances, the reasons he gave; but because it provided him a convenient excuse, at that time as well as now, to abandon her! In any case, how could she know now?

The hour of wood-wind music is over. Akin has concluded several thoughts—thoughts about herself, thoughts about Alex, thoughts which up until now she has been afraid to think or to speak openly.

She stands the instrument near the window

and sits down at the circular table to write **Alex** a last and final letter.

The 31st

Dear Alex,

I have thought over clearly in my mind what it is that holds us from one another. You write me that you have found a way of sending for me. I do not believe this. I mean, I do believe that at the moment when you were writing, "I have found a way to send for you," it was true. Yet, I am convinced that you have imagined this. Just as you have imagined that bringing a child into this world is a strange, imagined contradiction. You have not really gained what you have searched for. You, like the guarding god, have trumped everything. While you played up to the passing woman, you had a love affair with faith behind the altar. And so we are lost in the end.

About your travels. You tell me that you will write a book. And there again, I am inclined to believe that your travel book will never be written. If you will stop a moment and think about these things, seriously, you will discover that deep down in your heart there is little or no desire for anything.— Your ego has control of you. So when you tell me to destroy our child, and then you offer me pleas of remorse while you continue living in a dream, I have no alternative but to think you totally mad. Furthermore, I cannot see that it is a question of financial circumstances that keeps us apart. But rather, it is a question of how much I mean to you. For you say that you love me more than I love you; I believe this to be the contrary of the fact. And so, I feel there is no force— a hold equal on both our parts—to give strength for continuing our relationship.

I believe that this letter will be clear to you. I shall not be writing to you again, nor do I wish to hear from you evermore.

Goodbye, Alex,
Akin

⤳ 2 AKIN AND PETER GIÓRGOS

Characters

Walter   *a small boy*

Ezra Arahk   *Akin's brother*

Harry and Nida   *a sculptor and his wife*

Peter Giórgos   *cousin of Alex*

Others

Tall girl, two short men   *intruders*

Man sitting on bench   *streetwalker*

Akin and Peter Giórgos

The door is closed and the key turns inside the lock. Akin wraps a silk band, a magenta necktie-shaped fabric, over and around her high collar. She walks downstairs, out into the street.

She carries a pencil-box purse. A letter addressed to Alex, a half slice of dried bread, and eighty cents in pennies wobble from one side to the other within the pencil box.

"Will I meet a friend who will invite me to lunch?" Akin automatically asks herself. And the thought quickly passes.

She walks two blocks directly ahead, four blocks to her right, then down a sloping hill which leads to the railway depot. She can see the huge clock of the church steeple just behind the station. Still only ten-fifteen. Akin walks the remainder of the street slowly, for it is early. And as she walks, she playfully presses her pencil-box purse lightly against the wire fence at her right, creating a drumming sound. . . .

When Akin enters the station, she still has seven minutes to wait for her train. After circling the waiting room several times, stopping idly at each of the double life-size photographs plastered half-way to the ceiling—the American Worker Today—Akin pauses, opens her pencil box and recounts her pennies. Finally she sits at the back of the station on a long, hardwood bench. The minutes pass slowly.

She stretches her legs out before her and leans back, resolved not to think about anything. Her eyes wander over the enlarged photographs to the ceiling above, which is painted brick color.

"Ugly ceiling," she says to herself just as a small boy approaches her, walking along on the seat of the bench.

The boy stops a few feet from Akin and stares at her with infantile open-mouthedness. He then brings his hands to his lips and begins

58

giggling mischievously. Akin straightens up in her pose, crosses her knees, takes the pencil box in one hand and places one wrist over the other on her lap. The boy points to Akin's stomach while still covering his mouth with one round, pink hand. He says: "I know what you've got," in a rhythmical voice.

Akin turns to him as though she has not seen him approach her, as though she had not heard him speak. Her movement is calculated and her eyes are only half open.

"What did you say, little boy?" says she.

"You can't fool me," says he abruptly. He holds his arms awkwardly and poses both feet the width of the bench. "You don't have to pretend with me, lady." He looks down at Akin and the expression on his face changes. He then speaks as though reciting a school poem: "My name is Walter. My age is eight years old. My mommy is a housewife. My daddy is a bread-truck driver." The boy smiles to himself. He is proud of his father who drives a bread truck. Akin ignores him, however.

The boy now leans forward and his face

59

comes within inches of Akin's ear. "My mommy says little boys like me have a right to know about those things. I'm seven years old already," says he, almost in a whisper. "Mommy says Daddy put six babies in her belly. Every summer Daddy puts a baby in Mommy's belly," he says.

Akin makes believe she doesn't know the boy is standing on the seat beside her.

"Look! Look!" says the boy. And he points to the first long bench at the front of the waiting room.

One, two, three, four, five. Five small children, each one slightly bigger than the next, sit quietly in a line. At the left of the tallest child sits a woman reading a *Love Story* magazine and wearing a pink and lavender net hat. Akin raises herself, mechanically turns right, walks to the ticket window and buys a one-way fare to Manhattan. Her eyes are still half closed.

Once on the train, Akin walks from coach to coach. In the last car there are a number of vacant seats. She chooses the one farthest away from the other passengers, and seats herself comfortably. As the train begins to move, she watches the dull landscape flicker by.

And ideas flicker through her mind: When I get off the train in Manhattan, I'll go directly to my brother's apartment. He is certain to be there at that hour. He usually sleeps until ten or eleven, and the remainder of the morning he idles about thinking of ideas for new dresses to design.

"Good morning, dear Brother," I'll say very casually. "I thought I'd drop in for a few minutes to see how you are doing."

He'll look at me in his usual superior manner. "I'm getting on fine," he'll say with one eyebrow raised. "But what brings you to town?" He will sit on the long, modern couch, still in his underwear, legs folded under him like a Buddha. "There's food in the frigidaire, if you're hungry," he will say.

"No thank you," I'll reply. "I just now finished a huge breakfast at Schwarz's. I thought I'd spend the day in town today and pay little visits here and there." He will know that I haven't had breakfast at all. He will insist that I go to the kitchen and help myself to the straw-

61

berries and cream. "I've really had breakfast," I'll tell him. "But I don't think I'll pass up the strawberries." He will follow me into the kitchen, and I'll ask him routine questions while he watches me eat. "Have you received any new commissions since I last saw you?" I will ask.

"My dear!" he'll proudly exclaim. He'll blow at his fingernails and extend his profile. "You are now the proud sister of Ezra Arahk, Incorporated: Designer and Costumer of the World's Most Smartly Dressed Women."

"Have you really opened your own shop this time?" I'll ask, as though it were the first time I had heard about the prospect.

"Yes, my dear," Ezra will say still holding his pose and brushing his nails on the strap of his undershirt. "And furthermore, I'm seriously considering having you in the business with me."

"Me? Ezra," I'll say in a delighted manner.

"Of course you!" Aren't you my lovely, talented, bright little sister who lives like a nun in a filthy room in Roselle, New Jersey?" He will then smile and take a biscuit from the cupboard. "I've decided that it's about time you gave up your degeneracy and get back on your feet. To be frank with you, my dear, it's terribly un-chic to be living like a taoist these days."

"Perhaps you are right, Ezra." I will not let him think I'm over-anxious, however. "I'd really like to come in on the dress shop with you; that is, if it ever materializes." I'll leave a few of the strawberries on the plate and look at him non-committally, face blank. "Ezra, I should tell you, I was planning to take on a job anyway. If you open the shop, that will be fine. Meanwhile, I thought it would be best to find something else—like playing oboe with an orchestra here in the city—while I'm still able to work."

Ezra will look at me skeptically. He'll follow me back into the living room and he will wait until I've placed several records on the phonograph. Then he'll say, "By the way, dear little sister, have you decided what you're going to do?"

"No, Ezra, I haven't decided as yet."

"Don't you think that if you don't decide very soon, there won't be any choice afterwards?"

63

"Yes, of course, I realize that. But I want to wait a week or so longer before doing anything definite. I want to see whether or not I can get work first. If possible, I want to keep the child."

"That's foolishness, Akin! You're very foolish," he will say as an angry brother. "If I've told you once, I've told you a thousand times that you should have taken care of the matter long ago. You don't really think, do you, that your transient, neurotic friend is ever going to return to you and claim the child?"

"No, Ezra. I'm not expecting him to return. I don't believe I honestly care whether he comes back or not. In any case I don't think about him anymore. I'm thinking only about myself, and about my child."

"You'll never straighten yourself out, if you don't get rid of it. I warn you, Akin!"

"Ezra. Please don't snap at me so. I simply came to pay a social call. If you don't want to see me as I am, I won't come around again," I'll say running into his arms as though about to burst into tears. We have had scenes like this often.

64

"I'm sorry, Akin," he will say then. "I guess you know what you are doing."

"I want you to help me, Ezra." I know that he will not reject my plan now. "I want you to introduce me to one of your clients."

"To one of my clients?" he'll echo, quite surprised. "Which client, Akin?"

"I don't recall her name," I'll say. But I shall mimic her voice and hold one arm out in the air, pretending I have a cigarette in my hand as she usually does. And he will know which one I mean. I'll say. "You know which one, Ezra. This one . . ."

He'll laugh loudly. "That old windbag connected with the Met?" he'll say.

"Yes. What's her name? You know. She can probably give me a couple of months' work with the orchestra, if you tell her you have a lovely sister who plays the oboe beautifully."

He will think to himself awhile, drumming a table with his elegant fingers. Then he'll look at me as though the idea were altogether his own. "Of course, in exchange for this little favor, Madame Waldbom," he'll say, bowing like a connoisseur at an art gallery, "I shall present you with the hat made of peacock feathers—for free! You old windbag—the hat you've asked me for so many times.''

And we'll both laugh triumphantly.

The sun has come out. A few minutes pass as Akin smiles at her reflection in the plate-glass window to her left.

Just then the boy who had spoken to her in the waiting room at Roselle is seen down the far end of the car. He slowly moves down the aisle, settling himself on the seat next to Akin. She is annoyed. What could he be wanting now? she asks herself. Akin gathers her skirt tightly under her legs and covers her stomach with her arms. The boy sits quietly and doesn't speak.

Five minutes pass.

At length the child pulls on the sleeve of her blouse, very gently. Akin does not stir from her blank stare toward the seat opposite them.

"Lady?" says the boy softly. "Can I sit here?"

Akin is silent.

"Lady?" says the boy a bit louder, thinking she hasn't heard him. "Can I sit here?"

"Yes, you may," says Akin without looking

at him. "You may sit there if you promise to be quiet."

"I'll be quiet," promises the boy. A tear floods his eyes as though someone was about to slap his face.

Akin is still feeling rather uneasy. She slides the top of her pencil box open and rearranges the objects within in neat piles. She is trying to clear her mind, so as to return to her own ideas.

"Lady?" begins the boy once more. "I've got to sit here because there isn't any more chairs in the coach where my mommy's at."

"All right, then. Sit there!" shouts Akin in an angry voice. She hopes that the boy now understands she doesn't want to have anything to do with him.

After a long silence, Akin reconsiders her feelings. She has been rude to the small boy, and unless she makes some friendly remark to him, she will be upset for the remainder of the day. Akin leans close to him to say pleasantly, "What's your name, little boy?"

He smiles. He is delighted. He is overwhelmed. Says he, "Put 'n tame, ask me again and I'll tell you the same," laughingly, jokingly.

Akin centers herself back at her own side of the seat. Now she is cross with herself for having asked the boy his name.

"What's your name?" asks he while moving over to lean on Akin's arm.

She ignores the boy, trying to recall the thoughts which she had developed before he came.

"Lady? What's your name?" says he louder.

Akin rubs her forehead nervously. She wants to block away the boy's question from her mind. "Akin Arahk," she says in a quick voice, as though just having been cross-examined.

"Funny name you've got," comments the boy, who has moved back to his side of the seat. He is determined to keep up a conversation with Akin for the remainder of the voyage. "Everybody says I've got a funny name, too." He looks down at his dirty hands. "But I don't care. My name's Walter—but I don't care. Some people's got funny names, and some people don't. I don't care though what they call people. My two brothers' names is Alfred and Willy. That's just as funny. Ain't it, lady?"

"Yes," says Akin, feeling rather silly for having become overly emotional. "Names really don't matter a great deal, you know. It's the people themselves who count."

"Names really don't matter a great deal," says the boy, repeating Akin's phrase. "My sisters are called Joanne, Mildred and Dizzy. But I don't care. Names really don't matter a great deal," parrots he, thinking that he has made a friend of Akin.

Akin looks over and smiles at the small boy. He smiles at her, moves nearer once more and places one hand under Akin's arm.

"You know," begins the boy in a profound tone, "You know, if I had a baby I wouldn't call it anything. I wouldn't call it anything until it was grown up. I'd let it call it's own name. That's what I'd do."

She is amused by what the boy has said. Akin looks down to her stomach, then faces the boy. "I believe your idea is entirely sound," she says. "Children should be allowed to choose names for themselves."

"Lady?" says he in the same pleading voice with which he had begun speaking to her, "Are

69

you going to let your baby choose its own name?"

"Yes. Of course I am. When my baby has grown up, I'll let it decide upon a name for itself."

"What are you going to call it until it grows up?" asks the boy, questioning himself as well as Akin.

"I don't know exactly," replies Akin. She thinks to herself a moment, then says, "If it's a boy, I'll call it Boy. If it's a girl, I'll call it Girl."

"That's right," says the boy, smiling at her inability to solve the problem. "But do you know if your baby is going to be a boy or a girl?"

Akin laughs. "I don't know just yet," she says, and suddenly wonders to herself, Is my baby going to be a boy or a girl?

"I'll bet your baby is going to be a girl," offers the small boy. "I bet if you let me feel your belly I can tell you if it's going to a girl or not."

What a strange thing for a child to say, thinks Akin. Isn't it rather premature for a child his age to want to feel my stomach, to feel my baby inside? Akin quickly glances about to assure herself that no one has heard their conversation. She then leans nearer the boy's face and says softly, "All right, Walter. You can feel my belly, if you really think you can tell whether I'm going to have a boy or a girl."

The small boy beams as though he had just won a candy-stick at the circus. With exaggerated gestures, he pulls back his sleeves and looks out the plate-glass window for a moment. Then his tiny hands approach her and he places them caressingly on Akin's stomach. He closes his eyes as he begins moving his fingers across one side, then the other, and pressing lightly each time. Akin feels rather foolish; yet she is quite moved by the seriousness with which the boy plays his game. His hands are like little butterflies.

"No. Not yet," says he. His eyes are still closed.

Akin relaxes in her seat and allows the boy all the time he wants. She is wondering what the small boy will say. Will it be a girl? Will it be a boy? Akin is wishing she will have a boy.

A boy is stronger. Should she find that she is unable to support herself and a child after it has arrived, it will be easier to let a boy go— easier than a girl. Girls are sensitive and weak about these matters. Boys always manage to survive the blow of discovering that they are alone in the world. Sometimes it is a good stimulus for them. They go off and become explorers, adventurers, seekers. I do hope he says it will be a little boy, thinks Akin finally.

The jarring of the train, the movement of the boy's searching fingers, thoughts of another day when other hands passed across her stomach in this same manner give Akin the impulses of passion. Her lips part slightly.

"I bet I can tell you now!" says he as he opens his eyes. He slides his hands away. "I was wrong the first time, but I bet I can tell you now."

Akin rises from the seat and takes her pencil box in her hands.

"Wait a moment," says she, patting the boy's head affectionately. "Wait 'till I come back and you can tell me then. I'll only be gone a moment."

The boy's round, blue eyes follow Akin's graceful movements as she walks to the end of the aisle and disappears within a door marked: Ladies.

At Forty-Third Street Akin turns up Lexington Avenue until she reaches the Fifties. She walks slowly up the seven flights of stairs to her brother's apartment. She reaches his door and presses the buzzer. She waits.

When there is no answer, she then knocks on the door several times and loudly calls out his name. No one is in. Akin takes a penny from her pencil box and places it in the keyhole. Her brother will know by this that she has been by and will return later. Then she leaves.

Out in the street once again, Akin crosses to Fifth Avenue, where she walks along in a leisurely manner admiring the window displays of expensive clothing shops. She decides to go downtown. And with her last ten cents she boards a downtown bus which takes her to Fourth Street.

"Will I meet a friend who will invite me to lunch?" she unconsciously asks herself.

Akin walks to Washington Square and seats herself on a gray-green bench near a poor, thin tree. For three-quarters of an hour she sits in the park breaking the dried bread into small pieces and feeding the bits to pigeons. As the birds flutter about her legs, their large breasts seeming to weigh them down and preventing them from flying away, Akin is momentarily reminded of Sir David Dove, of his sister Dorothea, and of the seven poodles.

"Come in, my dear," says Sir David, who is a slender man with a prominently beaked nose. "Don't mind the babies. They are quite harmless."

"Is this our dear Akin Arahk of whom Alex has spoken so many times?" screams a woman's voice in the next room. "Please do forgive me, my dear, I shall be with you in a minute."

"I'm terribly sorry to be late," says Akin, who was obliged to walk from the station to the hotel and who has only enough money in her purse to buy a return ticket to Roselle. "I had difficulty in finding the place," says she.

"There you are! Didn't I tell you this beastly place was impossible to find?" shouts Sir David to his eldest sister, Dorothea.

"Oh, my poor dear," says Dorothea, coming out of the bedroom and holding out her arms to greet Akin. "You poor darling! We should have sent a car out to fetch you," says she. Dorothea is plump and middle-aged.

"Please don't think about it," says Akin, who is rather surprised at the outlandish gown the woman is wearing. "Next time I'll know my way."

The poodles have scattered themselves, each one on an eighteenth-century chair. Akin looks around the room to find a vacant seat.

"Aren't they simply adorable?" squeaks Dorothea in her high-pitched and British voice. "I simply love the dear creatures. They're the only children I have in the world. My husband was such a stuffy old thing, he couldn't bear an animal in the house—let alone children. The day I brought these babies home, he marched out of the house and never returned."

75

"Now Dorothea, my dear," says Sir David, who is putting on his overcoat, "let's wait to tell Miss Arahk all about ourselves another time. Can't you see that the girl is famished from hunger?"

A moment later:

"Akin! What are you doing here?" asks a hoarse voice breaking in on Akin's daydream. "Thought you were supposed to be living over in New Jersey?"

It is Harry speaking. His wife, Nida, is with him. And they are both wearing turtle-neck sweaters. "Hello, Harry! Hello, Nida!" says Akin, as though just rescued from a perplexing nightmare. "You both look so lovely, standing there staring at me."

"Greetings, beautiful," says Nida, who is from Detroit and who somehow doesn't belong with Harry and the group of sculptors whom he knows. "What's the latest news from Palestine?" says she.

"Drop dead," says Harry to Nida from the corner of his mouth. He is always scolding her for speaking out of turn. Harry sits down on one side of the bench, next to Akin. "Is everything going to turn out okay?" he asks sympathetically.

"Why certainly, Harry," Akin replies, smiling. "I'm moving back to the city soon. My brother is getting me a job with the Metropolitan." She has known Harry for several years and has had many exciting talks with him about art, music, writing—as well as about her personal life. "Did your exhibit take successfully?"

"I don't want to talk about it," says he bitterly. "The papers panned it, said I had a style but *so did Henry Moore*. Isn't that a corn-ball thing to say?"

"I'm sorry, Harry," says Akin, who has always admired his work. "Did you make any gold?" she asks in the vernacular she knows will please him.

"Christ! Everyone that came to see the things were the cats from around here. A few squares floated in now and then, but they wouldn't touch the stuff. I had to hock my tweed suit to pay the bill at the gallery. But I'll make it up when I get another order for flower pots."

"Aren't the ceramics going either?"

"You don't think the squares really appreciate ceramics, do you? If I can sell one ash-tray a week, I'm doing good business. It'll pick up, though. It's got to. We're practically starving."

"Yeah, beautiful," breaks in Nida. "We're practically starving," says she pleadingly. "You don't suppose you can loan us a couple fins, eh?"

"Drop dead," says Harry again. "Don't mind her, Akin. We've got a can of pork and beans someplace up there in the loft." Harry yawns, stands up to leave, then says, "Are you hungry, kid?"

"No, Harry," says Akin. She is grateful to him for asking. "I can always go to my brother's place. I'm sorry I don't have money with me or I'd be glad to help you out."

"Don't worry about us, Akin. We'll always make it one way or another." Harry takes Nida by the arm. "We've got to cut, Akin. Maybe we'll be seeing you around, eh?" says he.

"Yes, Harry. I'm to be living in town any day, now that I'm getting a job. I'll see you around soon."

"Goodbye, beautiful," says Nida, who is surprised that they are leaving so quickly. "Come up and see us if you ever get hungry. You know where we live, eh?"

"Drop dead!" says Harry, and pulls her out of the park.

An unshaven old man sits on the bench opposite Akin, across the walkway. He is wearing two shirts, two waistcoats, and two pairs of trousers. His pockets are bulging, over-stuffed with personal belongings. He crosses one knee over the other, unbuttons one waistcoat, and draws a folded newspaper from one of his pockets. He begins reading the Racing section.

Akin shoos the pigeons aside and walks over to the old man.

"Excuse me," says she politely, as though she were interrupting a theologian meditating on his Bible. "I wonder if you would mind letting me see the Classified Ads?"

The old man looks up. He is amazed to see the young girl speaking to him. He turns and looks behind himself to see whether it might be someone else she is speaking to. There is no one behind and he has heard Akin's words distinctly. He then looks at Akin from head to foot. "I can't afford it," he says abruptly, pulling the paper up to cover his face.

Excuse me, Akin says to herself and returns to her bench, I guess the man does have a right to keep his Classified Ads section, if he wants. She concludes with the thought that he might have misunderstood, then dismisses him from her mind.

The pigeons return to flock about Akin's feet. She doesn't have any more bread crumbs, however; so she takes one of the pigeons on her lap and strokes its back. She thinks about the small boy on the train. And this thought leads her to pick up again the conversation she had imagined took place with her brother.

"Ezra," I'll say, as though turning a new leaf in life, "If Madame Waldbom gets me the job playing with the Met, I'm going to save money, have the child, and later leave America."

"Leave the States?" he'll say, and thinking that it might be a good idea for himself, "London, Paris, Rome—hmm," he'll say approvingly. He has never been to Europe, and the prospect of having a lavishly decorated apartment in one of the European capitals has always intrigued him.

"I can live on a small farm outside of Paris until the child is older. By that time I'll have arranged for a job playing the oboe with a company touring Europe."

Ezra will turn on me violently. "You're not thinking of following that psychopathic Alex all the way to Siberia, are you?"

"No, Ezra. Of course not! I told you once: I don't want to have anything to do with him again. In fact I've got a letter right here in my purse telling him that we are through for good. I have no intention of ever seeing him again in my life."

"If that's the case, perhaps you and I could leave for Europe together," he'll say, becoming quite excited about the idea of having French love affairs.

"No, Ezra. I want to go alone."

I shouldn't have said that to him, thinks Akin to herself. He feels rejected now. "What I really mean, dear Ezra, is that I don't want to have you feeling I'm your responsibility."

81

"Don't give me any of that stuff!" he'll shout at me, having caught me retracking my real meaning. "Everytime I try to help you, it's always wasted. You're a selfish little girl, Akin! Face it yourself!"

Ezra and I have had scenes like this often, thinks Akin.

It begins to rain and the pigeons fly away. Akin notices that the old man who was sitting across from her is gone. He has left part of his newspaper on the bench. She runs over, picks it up, and makes a roof out of it to shield herself from the rain. He has left the Classified Ads section. Akin walks out of the park through the rain which now falls in a heavy downpour. Five minutes later Akin mounts three flights of stairs to a cold-water flat on Prince Street. She stands for a moment outside a door which is painted yellow, while she brushes the raindrops from her shoulders. Placed at the center of the yellow door, a small, white card mounted with adhesive tape reads: *12½ * Body * Block * P. Giórgos*. P. Giórgos is a friend of Akin's, and is Alex's cousin. She knocks.

The door opens immediately. There stands Giórgos in a faded, purple shirt unbuttoned to his waistline. His hair is thick, black, and curly. He is five years older than Akin; they are the same height.

"Hi, baby," he says to her in a musical voice. "Don't stand there, baby. Come in and shut the door."

Akin walks into the small, untidy cold-water flat, but she doesn't say a word. Giórgos realizes that something besides the rain has upset her.

"Look, baby," he says, turning a large canvas which has been facing the wall, "look at this clown I've just finished."

Akin has moved over to the drawing-table and is making squares with India black ink on a clean sheet of paper. She looks around to the painting Giórgos is holding. She squints.

"Peter, haven't I seen that one before?"

"No, baby, not this one," says he. Giórgos is disheartened by her comment. "I just finished this one this morning. You're thinking of that one—" says he, as he points to the wall behind Akin to a painting of another clown which is hanging without a frame.

Akin glances quickly, then returns to her scribbling. She is still standing and doesn't speak.

Giórgos feels rather uneasy. He doesn't know what to say that will cheer Akin. Nor what to say that will cheer himself. Giórgos is ordinarily very lively and exuberant whenever Akin calls on him. "I got a commission to block-in for a friend doing window-display," says he, forcing a smile. "Starting tomorrow. Isn't that great?" He cannot tell whether the news pleases her or not.

"I'm glad for you, Peter," says Akin, still looking at the previously clean sheet of paper she is marking.

Giórgos unexpectedly dashes into the kitchen. The water he has had on to boil is overflowing on the gas jet. He takes a dirty towel hanging over a frying pan and proceeds to clean the mess as best he can. "Would you like a cup of good, hot coffee?" he says to Akin through the wall.

Akin isn't drawing squares any longer. She is watching the rain. It occurs to her that she has left her window open in Roselle. "Thank

84

you," she says finally. "I'd love one if there is some already made."

Two hand-painted cups are brought down from a shelf which is overcrowded with bread, seven small spice jars, boxes of rice, pancake flour, cornflakes, raisins, and a bottle of vinegar. Giórgos holds the cups to his face while pouring them half full with hot water. He then puts a spoon of nes-café in each cup.

"Sorry, baby," says he coming out of the kitchen and holding the cups out before him, "those bastards who share this place with me didn't leave sugar this morning."

Akin takes one cup from him and holds it under her chin with both hands so as to warm her neck. She is thinking about Harry and Nida. They really suit each other quite well in the long run, Akin thinks to herself. She then leans against the window board.

"Have you heard from Alex lately?" asks Giórgos, who is seated on the floor and is anxious to stimulate conversation.

Akin turns to him furiously and speaks to the wall above Giórgos's head. "I haven't come here to speak about Alex!"

85

Giórgos, remaining seated on the floor with his head bent down, finishes his coffee quietly. He thinks about Akin's remark. It occurs to him where it was that he had heard the same phrase before.

"What were you just thinking about?" asks Akin in a manner of apology for having created a tension between them.

"As a matter of fact, baby, I was thinking about you," says he slowly. He is searching his mind for a way of speaking about Alex without provoking Akin's temper. Unpremeditated words begin flowing out of his mouth. "I was thinking about you just before you knocked on the door. I was wondering if you would consider living here in the apartment with me, if I could get rid of the two guys and make enough money to feed us both."

"What an insane idea," says Akin, setting her cup down on the sheet of paper so that it covers the squares. Whenever she has been angry, upset, tired, embarrassed, depressed in the past, she would take advantage of Giórgos's weak character to reprimand him for making obscure statements without thinking first. And now she

86

sulks at him. "Don't you think that that's a rather impulsive suggestion at this point?"

"Well, baby," says he, trying to make good his hasty declaration, without seeming totally ridiculous, "I don't see that it's such a bad idea. At least you wouldn't have to be paying rent or eating out all the time. And there are a lot of people who come up here, you know. You can have some company once in awhile."

"Peter Giórgos! Sometimes I wonder about you!" Akin says, lifting one eyebrow like her brother.

"But why not?" insists Giórgos, who is looking up at her and is totally bewildered. His offer doesn't seem so very insane to him, after all.

"Because I don't want to see a lot of people! for one thing. Did that ever occur to you?" says Akin bending down to his face with her hands on her hips. She continues to sulk at him and lifts her eyebrows even higher. Her face is red.

Giórgos spreads his lips and reveals his teeth pressed tightly together. His face smiles up as though just having been caught using a double mirror to gaze at his profile or to comb the back of his hair. "I guess I'm a silly dope," says he, barely parting his teeth.

Just then a knock comes at the door.

Before Giórgos can reach it, however, a figure hidden under a broken, open umbrella dashes in. It is Nida. And she is soaked from the rain.

After she places the umbrella upside down in the center of the room, she looks back and forth between Akin and Giórgos. Nida imagines that she has walked in on something intimate.

"Hi! beautiful," she says to Akin. "Hi! beautiful," she says to Giórgos. "I ain't busting in on something, am I?"

"No, not at all," says Giórgos. In one way he is pleased that Nida appeared just then; in another way, he is not. "Here, let me take your umbrella, baby," he says taking the umbrella by the handle as though it were a snake. He carries it to the kitchen.

"Well I'll be damned!" Nida carries on. "Didn't we just see you in the park today? I was just telling Harry right after we left you that I bet we'd see beautiful again today. Well,

I'll be damned! Isn't that just like a woman's intuition? Now who would think that I knew we'd really see you again today? You never know, see? I was telling Harry right after we got to the loft that beautiful had better get out of the park or she'll go floating down a sewer, 'cause it's raining like hell. You never know, see? Well I'll be damned. Here you are!"

Giórgos returns from the kitchen with a dirty towel and begins drying Nida's dress from the back. "What can I do for you, baby," says he pleasantly. "I'm broke, if that's what Harry sent you for."

"Don't be a harpy, beautiful," says Nida, holding her arms above her head in the attitude of a ballerina. "Everytime I come over here you think it's for gold. And all we want is a dish of lard." She turns to face Giórgos, who allows her to continue. "That's what I get for coming all the way over here in the rain. Insults! I was just telling Harry that I bet that's what you'd think I came over for. Well I'll be damned! I've guessed everything that happened to us today. This morning it was the spoon that fell on the floor. I told Harry we'd get a

89

letter. And what do you think? Sure enough. We got a postal card. It was from that guy Alex. Do you know Alex?" she asks turning to Akin.

Akin crosses her knees, folds her hands, and leans forward. She looks up at Nida with her eyes half closed. "Yes, as a matter of fact, I do," says she. Giórgos moves quickly to the kitchen to get the lard.

"You do? Well I'll be damned! You see? Small world, eh? Just think, there we were sitting, minding our own business; the spoon falls, and we gets this card all the way from Africa. You'd think that a place like Africa was all the way to Timbuctoo from the looks of the crazy stamp. You never know. Small world, eh? Harry says Timbuctoo *is* in Africa. I didn't know that. I thought it was somewhere in Arizona or Wyoming, you know, out West in the desert.

"What did the postal card say?" interrupts Akin, without wanting to seem especially interested.

"The card? Well, I don't know," says Nida, making herself comfortable on the mattress next to Akin. "I didn't get to read the damned thing. Harry grabbed it right out from under my nose. What do you think of a husband like that? If I had the money, I'd go back to Detroit. Who the hell wants a husband that won't even let you look at a postcard? You'd think it had dirty pictures on it, or something. I should have married a guy like beautiful. Eh, Giórgos? There's a real husband for you. He does everything about the house. He waits on you. He'd even buy you a new dress if you wanted. Wouldn't you, beautiful?" she shouts toward the kitchen.

"Sure, baby. Anything," replies Giórgos, who has only heard the last words she said. He is emptying one of the jars of spice to put the lard in.

"That's a husband for you, I say. Just ask him, and you get it like *that*—," Nida snaps her fingers. "I asked Harry to buy me a girdle last week. I'm sagging all over the place . . . Look at this old thing I'm wearing," says she lifting her skirt, "it looks like a sack for potatoes . . . Anyway, I asked him to buy me a dress last week and he just smacked me across the mouth and walked out of the house. Didn't say a word to me. And stayed out all night. Harry's that way, though. I've got to forgive him sometimes. You've got to expect those things if you're married to an eccentric."

"He didn't read the card to you by any chance?" asks Akin. She realizes that Nida will not mind tracing back her thoughts about Timbuctoo.

"Why sure he did. I should have told you that." She points to her chin with one finger and reflects for a moment. Then she says as an introduction, "I only met the guy once, you know. He's one of these crackpots. Runs around with his hair cut off like a turtle. And the way he talks you'd think he was somebody. Harry introduced him to me one day we were at Jimmie's place. This guy Alex was there with some chick. Now see? I can't even remember who was there with him."

Akin is rather disgusted with Nida and has just about given up hope of hearing what Alex had written to Harry. She walks over to the window and looks down to the street below. Three little girls are running about barefooted in the rain.

"Giórgos?" says Nida, still pondering to herself and walking into the kitchen, "who was that chick we saw with Alex at Jimmie's place last year?"

"It was Akin," says Giórgos almost inaudibly, thumbing his finger toward the next room.

"Well I'll be damned. What do you think of that?" says Nida, returning to the mattress on the floor. "It was beautiful."

Just then the door opens. A tall, blonde girl walks in with two, short, Italian-looking men behind her. The two men have their hands in their pockets and appear like hold-up men.

Nida turns to them and smiles. With her hand out. She walks over to the tall blonde and says, "Hi, beautiful. My name's Nida. What's yours?"

As the group begins introducing themselves to Nida, Akin walks by them without saying a word and goes into the kitchen. "Peter! Who are those people out there?"

Giórgos finishes wrapping the jar of lard with wax paper from the bread. Then he takes a quick look into the next room. "I don't know.

I guess they're friends of the two guys that live here," says he perplexed.

"Let's go out, Peter," says Akin, who has noticed through the small window above the sink that the rain has stopped outside. "The rain has stopped."

"Out?" says Giórgos. He looks at Akin and sees that she has become furious. "Sure, baby. We can go to the automat, if you want."

They leave the apartment without letting the others know. Nida, the tall blonde, and the two, short Italians are gathered on the mattress, talking intensely.

As Akin and Giórgos reach the bottom of the stairs, Harry comes rushing toward them excitedly. "Where's my wife?" he says as though someone has gone off with her.

"She's upstairs," replies Giórgos.

Before Akin has a chance to ask Harry about the postal card, he races up the stairs.

At the automat nearest Prince Street, Akin and Giórgos order coffee. Akin has decided to speak to Peter about Alex.

94

"When's the last time you heard from Alex?" she asks suddenly.

"Alex?" says Giórgos. He feels guilty, for no apparent reason. "Let's see. I guess it was about a month or two ago." He pauses, then says, "But why?"

"For various reasons." Akin opens and closes her pencil-box purse. "For one thing, I'm through with him."

Giórgos remains silent, while a series of explosive thoughts rush to his mind. Why? What happened? Does Alex know about the baby? Did he write and say the child wasn't his? Did he say that *he* was through? Is he coming back?

"I can't explain it all to you just now, Peter. But I will another time. The important thing is this—" Akin becomes nervous and Giórgos orders another coffee. "I want to get a job. I want to work for awhile, so that I can have money to keep the child."

"Oh? You're going to keep the baby?" says he, not knowing what reaction is best.

"Yes, I'm keeping the baby, and I'm also going to leave the country."

95

"You're going away?" says Giórgos, even more uncertainly.

"Naturally. I've got to leave now. But I must get a job so that I can afford the child. I thought of asking my brother to help me, but I know that he won't be pleased with the idea I have in mind." Akin finishes her coffee and looks at Giórgos with a demanding appeal. "I want you to help me, Peter."

"Me?" says he.

"If you're going to be a complete idiot about it, I might as well stop talking right now."

"What do you mean? You know I'll do anything I can for you. But I don't know what there is I can do."

"I don't know exactly myself," says Akin, thinking to herself, "but I must confide in someone, and you're the only one I can trust right now."

"Sure, baby," says Giórgos who beams at the idea that he is being entrusted with Akin's secrets. "I'll do anything you want."

Akin takes a cigarette from Giórgos' pocket and lights it with exaggerated complacency. "Did you ever meet these British friends of

Alex's?" she asks as though speaking to a total stranger.

"Who? Those mad Doves?" asks Giórgos. He leans back and amuses himself while thinking about them. "Did they show you the picture they took of Alex?"

"They took a picture of Alex?" replies Akin.

"Akin, my dear, we did manage to get a photograph of Alex when we saw him in Morocco," says Sir David, as they are returning to the hotel. "Whenever I get everything unpacked, I'll find the picture and show it to you. The next time you come to visit us perhaps? You will be coming back soon, won't you?"

"Of course I will," says Akin, who has been depressed from the moment she opened the door, met the poodles, met Sir David, and met his sister Dorothea. "I shall drop by very soon," says she, having already forgotten about the photograph. Akin is determined never to see the British visitors again.

"What a picture!" says Giórgos. I'm telling you, Akin, it's the most fantastic, unbelievable

97

picture in the whole world. I tried to get the thing from them, but they said it was the only copy they had.

"Well, for heaven's sake," says Akin, "it couldn't have been *that* extraordinary. And besides, couldn't they at least have offered to let you make a copy from theirs?"

"I guess I didn't think about asking them at the time," says Giórgos, visualizing the strange photograph of his cousin that he had seen.

"Here, Peter darling," says Dorothea poking the photograph of Alex under his nose, "perhaps this will make you laugh. Actually, we had a frightful time taking it. When we asked Alex to pose for us, he stormed like a wild boar."

"Is this Alex?" says Giórgos, squinting his eyes and trying to recognize his cousin. "Are you sure this is Alex?"

"Why of course it's he, silly boy," says Dorothea, taking the photograph back and holding it under the lamp so that she might make certain she has shown the right picture.

"Well," says he, "my cousin has never looked like *that* before."

"Why what do you mean, Peter Giórgos? This is an excellent likeness of Alex." Dorothea places the photograph away between letter K and L in her large address book. "I admit, we had a beastly time catching him unaware of our Brownie. But we did succeed. This picture is exactly as we have known him. Come to think of it, I still don't know why he was so violently against having a photo taken. Isn't that peculiar?"

"If I looked like that, I'd violently refuse also," says Giórgos. He is still not convinced that the photograph is of his cousin.

"A bit eccentric he was about his hair. I've never in all my life seen a young man with such long hair. And it doesn't look natural—the outer layers are bleached by the sun, you know. And the cave. *That,* my dear, was too much! And his cane. Poor Alex, we told him so many times to rid himself of that filthy old stick of a cane. He was decent enough, however, to keep quite clean the Moroccan robe in which he draped himself."

"You mean that the snapshot was really of Alex?" says Giórgos, trying to imagine what his

99

cousin's appearance was like before leaving.

"Yes, of course, I've told you that a dozen times. The picture you saw is a photograph that David and I took of Alex in Morocco."

"Will you please stop for a minute acting like a new-born child over a silly photograph," says Akin. She is angry with herself for not having seen the Doves just one more time, so that she herself could have seen the photograph. She changes the subject. "I must find work, Peter. We've got to figure out some way to get me a job."

"You wouldn't want to wait on tables, would you?" says Giórgos, rejecting the idea himself.

"No. I couldn't do anything like that for very long now. It would wear me out before I had a chance to save anything."

"I guess you're right. The only reason I thought of it was because my godfather has a hot-dog joint near Harry's loft."

"What I would really like to do is to get a job playing oboe. Do you know any musicians?"

"Musicians?" says he, thinking to himself and recalling the three months that he was being sponsored in New Mexico. "Yes, Akin, I know a guy who plays the 'cello. And he's loaded with money."

"Do you think we can find him today?" asks Akin.

"I don't know, but we can try. This guy is so rich that he could probably get you a job playing at the Metropolitan, if you got on the good side of him. His grandfather was a famous German composer back in eighteen something or other."

"How can he be very rich, and play the 'cello?"

"Oh, he doesn't play the 'cello for a living. It's just a pastime for him. He's got a wild apartment on lower East Third Street."

"Peter!" says Akin, feeling that he has gotten his story mixed up with another person— probably someone who was the New York representative of a plastic button manufacturer out West. "East Third Street is the dumpiest district in town."

"I know that," says Giórgos. He is still beaming, for he knows that for once he will triumph over an obstacle. "This guy took one of those old, dilapidated warehouses and had the whole building done over. You wouldn't believe you were in the same part of town, once you get into the building . . . at least that's what a friend tells me. I've only been by. I haven't gone in yet."

"Can we go there now?" asks Akin.

"Sure, baby," says Giórgos, leaning back and taking out a cigarette. "Let's have another cup of coffee and we'll go."

Peter and Akin ride a bus to East Third Street. From the bus stop they walk four blocks East, crosstown. At length they reach the building where the 'cellist lives. The building is markedly different from others in the district: it has been renovated.

At the entrance Giórgos says, "I'm not going up, Akin."

"Why not?" says she. "Isn't this the right place, after all?"

"Sure it is," says he, while he cracks his fingers nervously. "But it's much better if you go up alone."

"I don't understand, Peter," says Akin, feeling that he is sending her on a wild goose chase. "If this is really the place, you should come up and introduce me to the man." She thinks a moment, then says, "You can leave right away, if you don't want to stay. Just introduce me. And when you see that everything is going smoothly, you can leave."

"But," says he hesitantly, "I don't feel like seeing him just now." Giórgos becomes red.

"That's silly! There's no sense in a total stranger walking into a man's apartment and expecting him to get her a job without his knowing her at all." She is furious with him. "Listen, Peter, if you honestly don't feel there's a chance of getting anywhere with this man, why don't you simply say so and not beat around the bush?"

"Sure there's the chance. There's a good chance. If you work it right, there's no limit to what you can get out of the guy. I'm telling you the honest t' God truth!"

"Then come up with me and let's get it over with. What's the matter? Are you on bad terms with him?"

"Hell no! We're still good friends. It's a funny relationship, though." He is embarrassed once more. "I may as well tell you—"

"I wish you would," says Akin. "Tell me the story, so that I can know if anything can be done here." She leans back against the wall at the entrance and crosses one foot over the other.

"Well, it's only that the last time I saw the guy was in Santa Fé." Giórgos waits.

"Well, so what?"

"So it was a funny set-up we had, you know?"

"No."

"Anyway, what happened was that I was superficially his little discovery. And I got fed up playing the part."

"So you walked out on him. Is that it?"

"So I walked out on him. Sure I did. I was being hounded by him everytime I'd go out to take a breath of air."

"But that's all understandable. What makes you so frightened of seeing him now?"

"Well, baby, out of sheer hell-desperation actually I took the liberty of hocking something of his so I could buy my ticket East."

"And you haven't seen him since?"

"And I haven't seen him since."

"All right. Let me handle it," says Akin, still determined at least to try the man out. She has had dealings with this type of person before —in connection with her brother Ezra's acquaintances—dress designers, show people, decorators, dancers, and just plain drunks whom he has brought to the apartment at one time or another. "Just give me a little slip with the 'cellist's name on it, and I'll go up myself."

Giórgos is pleased that Akin has decided to go up alone. He writes the name of the man Akin is to see on the back of a used envelope. Just as Akin looks over his shoulder, he says, "Just a moment. I might as well write a little note while I'm at it." Akin waits.

At the lower corner of the envelope Giórgos writes a number of words. He then reads it to himself, smiles, and hands it to Akin. "That should be enough."

"One more thing, Peter," says Akin in a tender voice, "leave me some money for the bus so I can get to my brother's place later."

"Sure, baby," says he, smiling and counting out his small change. "Will fifty cents be enough?"

Akin nods, and Giórgos hands her the money. "Will I be seeing you later?" he asks, hoping that she will let him know what the 'cellist has to say.

"Of course, Peter. I'll come to your place after I have supper with my brother. And I'll tell you all about your 'cellist friend."

As Akin begins reading the envelope, Giórgos walks away. "Bye, Akin!" he calls back.

Akin looks up and waves to him. "Bye, Peter!" she shouts. Then Alex's cousin turns the corner and Akin is left at the entrance to the renovated building, reading what he has written:

On one side: *Ludwig von Riefenbach* *D4

On the other: *Akin Arahk is a brilliant oboist who is in need of some advice about her music. Please help her if you can. Thank you.*

P. Giórgos

❧§ 3. AKIN AND LUDWIG
VON RIEFENBACH

Characters

Ludwig von Riefenbach   *'cellist*

Others

Man in black suit   *servant*

Akin and Ludwig von Riefenbach

A bald-headed man wearing a gray flannel suit opens the door. He glances at Akin from head to foot, questions himself for a moment, then makes a low bow which is an indication for Akin to enter. Akin holds her pencil box with both hands as she proceeds slowly, gracefully, down a long, narrow corridor. Her eyes, darting from left to right as she seems to glide along, take in the elegantly hand-painted window shades with which the hall windows are decorated. They are Japanese landscapes. The man in the gray suit follows lightfootedly behind.

When Akin reaches the end of the narrow hall, she finds that it continues on even further to the right. The second leg of the entranceway is wider, however, and tall glass windows insulate it from open roof gardens on either side.

The gardens are composed in a series of sections of low, clipped hedges expertly divided by miniature footpaths and artificial streams. A single willow tree is in each section, while here and there a small bridge is arched over the streams of clear, green water. These, in turn, open to ponds where countless little fishes swim. The fish are gold, silver, pink, and black.

Ahead of her is an arched doorway opening into a dark room. Akin stops at the archway, turns and waits for the man who is behind her. He is walking slowly. Occasionally he stops, admires the gardens on either side, and then continues walking along with his hands behind his back and still looking out through the glass wall. When he is by her side again, Akin hands him the envelope.

He reads the message carefully, reads the name and address on the reverse side, takes a white silk handkerchief from his sleeve, sneezes several times, then looks Akin over from head

110

to foot as though suddenly she had appeared before him.

"I am Ludwig von Riefenbach," says he, holding out a fragile hand to Akin and bowing his head slightly. "Won't you please come in?" He waves his other hand toward the darkened room. A chill runs through Akin as she feels the smoothness of his palm. And just then a light catches a superior and exceptionally large emerald he is wearing on his little finger. The ring seems to reflect the entire garden in its depths.

But Akin enters the room, proceeds to the center, and stands patiently in the dark while von Riefenbach pulls a cord at the windows. A flood of light fills every corner of the room as drapes are drawn open to reveal another wall of glass facing the garden.

"Won't you please make yourself comfortable over there?" invites the bald-headed man in a gracious manner. He points to a large arm-chair which has cushions made of a coarse, wool fabric woven by hand. The armchair is gray, and directly beside the chair is a low floor-table painted mauve. Akin walks over, cautiously sits on the arm of the sofa-chair, and loosens the band of the blue and white shirt from around her throat. She is facing the garden.

The slender man faces the glass wall also, folds his hands behind his back once more, and seems to fall into meditation as though he were the only person about in the oval-shaped room. Akin has a feeling that the room has a high ceiling, yet she doesn't dare lift her eyes from the garden. She is intrigued by the meeting.

"How is dear Peter?" he asks at length. His voice is penetrating and his words seem to echo back three or four times through the stillness of the apartment.

A silence prevails again. Akin waits a moment, then says, "Quite well, as a matter of fact." Her voice is low and soft. A curious peacefulness descends about her at the sound of her own voice. Quietly she meditates on the aspects of sound and color, as though she were in a dream. The rain out of doors begins sprinkling lightly, to shadow the intricate garden patterns with patches of green, lavender, pink and silver, and black. "He got a job, just this morning, doing window display," says she in the same soft voice.

"How nice, poor creature," says von Riefenbach, as though he were speaking of some other person—someone who might have designed the garden through the glass wall, with rain. "He has such a brilliant gift at painting. He deserves recognition, you know. Good for him," says he, lifting his eyebrows slightly.

An ethereal aura has enveloped von Riefenbach's head, and Akin now stares at him. She is wondering where she has seen him before. His eyes are deeply set back in his skull; and the bone structure of his cheeks protrudes, to hollow back as though modelled by a sculptor. His ears are small and his bare head is perfectly rounded so that his ball crown does not appear conspicuous. This only adds to his fascinating appearance. A learned man, whose graceful contours have ripened just at his approach to the afternoon of life, thinks Akin to herself.

"May I offer you some tea?" he asks with a faint smile as he turns to Akin. "It will only take a minute to prepare."

"Yes, I'd love some," says Akin, assuming her

far-away attitude with her eyes half closed. "That is, if it won't be too much trouble?"

"Of course not, my dear. I'm always delighted to have someone about the house at tea time. It is such a refreshing ritual," says he. "One usually feels slightly hungry at this hour. Don't you agree?" says von Riefenbach, walking to the other end of the room and disappearing through strings of many-colored, jingling beads.

"Yes," says Akin half-aloud, as she is left alone in the room. She makes herself comfortable in the sofa-chair, then says to herself, "One usually feels hungry at this hour."

The oval room is decorated with a taste for calmness, for space, for pastel colors and pure, subtle lines. A low fireplace without mantle or other décor is centered opposite the wall of glass. Two oblong-shaped couches lead from the fireplace, on either side, to the center of the room. The couches are like lonely, gray clouds floating silently in the large room-space, thinks Akin to herself. And two lamps with large, plain shades rest on small, oriental tables which have been placed on each side of the door hung with beaded string.

Just then a small, heavy-set man with white hair comes through the beaded door. He is carrying a large, round silver tray. He is wearing a black suit. He places the tray on the low table next to Akin's chair, bows courteously to her, and walks away with soft, quick steps. On the tray there are delicate cups and saucers of Chinese porcelain painted in flower designs.

The tea is served. Akin has concluded that von Riefenbach is no longer interested in Giórgos, his art, or his welfare. She imagines that Peter was just one more stone in this man's turning of stones. Had Giórgos been another person altogether, it would have been the same —another stone turned. It does not matter to Akin, however, that von Riefenbach should be so detached from people whom he has known. She is intrigued by von Riefenbach for more personal reasons.

His head is not naturally bald, and although he is twice Akin's age, he is still young. He has shaven off his hair, Akin decides as she finishes her tea.

Why is this? she asks herself. Had he caught some incurable disease during one of his travels to the Orient? Obviously he had been to the Orient. Maybe it was in Ceylon that he acquired the habits of some esoteric cult whose embodiment in philosophy dealt with rituals such as keeping one's head bald.

Curiously, Akin is reminded of Alex. Alex's hair was always short, short and brushed flat against his skull. In the dream which he had told her, remembers Akin, his hair had grown long—and this meant that he was well and happy? Akin looks at von Riefenbach now and sees the complete contradiction between his philosophy and Alex's.

"I understand that you play the 'cello," says Akin politely.

"Yes," he says to her, all the while standing up and facing the glass wall. It would seem that he wants to speak to someone outdoors. "I do play a bit."

Von Riefenbach has read Giórgos's message. He knows that Akin is an oboist. He will question her about this when he is ready. Perhaps

116

he will not speak to her about it at all. Akin decides not to bring Peter's message to his attention, unless he provokes the discussion. She has lost interest in her original motive for having come to the apartment on East Third Street. Akin feels a strange familiarity toward von Riefenbach. And she finds she is somewhat frightened by her own emotions. Everything else—thoughts, people, places, to her, for the moment, seem insignificant.

From where he is standing, von Riefenbach can reach over and pull the drape cord. Akin realizes that he is considering that.

He waits a moment. She remains silent. And then he pulls the cord which closes the drapes half way across the glass wall.

From where she is sitting, it becomes impossible for Akin clearly to distinguish objects about the room, and the bald-headed man is only a hazy image standing to the left of her. Akin makes herself comfortable on the sofa. She is obsessed by her host's strange personality and yet, now, she feels quite calm and relaxed. He, on the other hand, seems to be quite unaware of her presence. She stares at him and feels that he has a vacant look in his eyes. He is looking out into the darkened garden. Von Riefenbach is not there with her, she feels.

As he stands there thus, he begins speaking with an Elizabethan voice:

> "No, No, No, No! Come, let's away to
>   prison;
> We two alone will sing like birds i' the
>   cage.
> When thou dost ask me blessing, I'll kneel
>   down
> And ask thee forgiveness. So we'll live,
> And pray, and sing, and tell old tales, and
>   laugh
> At gilded butterflies, and hear poor rogues
> Talk of court news; and we'll talk with
>   them, too.
> Who loses and who wins; who's in, who's
>   out;
> And take upon 's the mystery of things
> As if we were God's spies; and we'll wear
>   out,
> In a wall'd prison, packs and sects of great
>   ones
> That ebb and flow by the moon. . . ."

And then he walks out of the room through the beaded door. Akin feels like a stone in the fireplace or a flank of the rectangular flower-box on the floor. She cannot move, but can only see and hear.

The gray-haired man enters and turns on one of the floor lamps at the archway. Then he disappears.

What has come over me? Akin says to herself as she hears a closet door open in the next room. What madness has duped me, that I should lose control over myself like this? I must get hold of myself. At once! Before the man returns.

Akin sits silently for a few minutes. Von Riefenbach has not returned. And she thinks. Why has he shaven his hair? Who is he? Why did he recite those lines? Can it be that he has cast a spell on me? Nonsense. How could that be? Yet how strange all this seems. And somehow I can associate my feelings now with a time and place I had felt this way before. Of course it is true. This has happened before. But where? When? says Akin to herself as she takes a cigarette from a transparent jar to her right and lights it.

119

The bald-headed man returns to the large room. He places a chair just at the place where he had been standing previously. He has a 'cello with him. Von Riefenbach sits quietly, meditating for a few minutes. Then, slowly, he draws a heavy, low note.

A farandole dance is begun.

Akin listens attentively while he plays. Breaks in the music cause unexpected thoughts to dart in and out of her mind.

How foolish I was, she thinks, for having taken seriously the things I thought while alone in the room.

How does one know when imagination plays tricks on reality?

How foolish I was, she thinks.

The piece is played to the end. Von Riefenbach meditates once more, a few minutes pass, and then he begins the same piece from the start.

And now, in contrast to the rhythm which seems to have doubled, Akin smokes deeply, slowly. She leisurely, gently, drops the ashes of her cigarette. The ashes fall and collect in the palm of her hand. The rhythm becomes steadily faster, while Akin's thoughts and actions become slower.

I feel comfortable sitting here like this. Why move? It will only disturb von Riefenbach's playing, she says to herself. Akin smokes and thinks lightheartedly. Had I the heart, the will, the mind, I would persuade myself to fall in love with this 'cellist. He would love me in time, in turn, and we would be happy together. Akin looks about the room briefly and then looks back at the middle-aged man playing the 'cello. Everything I want in the world is here in this room, she thinks. I would not find it necessary to search. I would not have need to go far for those things which would satisfy me in my life. If I should marry this 'cellist, I would not need to go any further. He would take my child, raise it as his own. He would want this. He would want to give his heritage, his name, to something which belonged to him. He would want the child.

But how can I be certain that he will consider all this? And Akin's thoughts wander from von Riefenbach.

"Beautiful creature, that Akin," says Sir David to his sister Dorothea, who is in her bedroom preparing to go to bed. Akin has returned to their door after having said good-night earlier in the lobby. Now she is standing at the door, listening, afraid to knock. She wants to ask Sir David to lend her enough money to pay her return fare to New Jersey.

"I grant you that," says Dorothea, as she gets into bed and takes a book in her hands. "But give her another month with that baby and she'll look a horror."

"Baby or no baby," replies Sir David good-humoredly, "she's a beautiful creature. Alex is a lucky boy. Wish I were in his shoes!"

"David!" shouts Dorothea throwing down her book, "such a ludicrous thing for you to say."

"What is so ludicrous about that?"

"Let's not discuss it!" says she, taking up her book once more, and then adding under her voice, "A man of your age taking a fancy to a young, pregnant girl. My word!"

"Now, Dorothea, stop getting so excited. It's only that you are envious of the poor creature that makes you think it such a ludicrous idea."

"Me? Envious? How dare you say such a thing, David. The nerve! It is perfectly outrageous of you to suppose that I would even bother myself about a young girl who goes off getting herself in such a condition."

"Dorothea, I'm beginning to think you are really jealous," says Sir David, knowing that he is upsetting his sister.

"Sir David Dove! We have had quite enough of such remarks," says she. But Dorothea is angry and is unable to commence her reading.

"Then why do you get so excited about it?" continues he. "Everyone knows that Akin and Alex will marry one day."

"I wouldn't be so sure of that. Whatever makes you think anyone would have her in that condition? He half-way off on the other side of the world." Once more she commences to read her book. But it is useless. "And I wouldn't be surprised to learn that it's *not* Alex's child in the end."

Just then Akin turns, walks to the elevator, presses the button, and waits.

The piece is played to the end. Akin walks to the fireplace and throws the end of her cigarette behind the screen. She turns around.

"Are you leaving, my dear?" asks von Riefenbach, still holding his bow in position of the last note. He is looking at the floor and his legs are trembling slightly.

"I don't know. It's getting late," says she, trying to decide what to do. "I must go soon."

"You would honor me by staying to have dinner here this evening." He does not move.

Have I bewitched him? Akin asks herself. Can this mean that what I had been dreaming a moment ago stands the slightest chance? What shall I say? Is he serious?

"I had promised my brother that I'd have supper with him this evening," says she, returning to the sofa-chair. "He'll be expecting me."

"I would very much like to have you stay. We are having *kouskous* for dinner," says von Riefenbach, hoping this will entice Akin to accept his invitation. "You can always phone your

124

brother from here, if you like—that is, if you wouldn't mind having dinner here with me."

"My brother probably isn't home yet. We'll wait awhile, and then see what he says on the phone." For herself, Akin hasn't yet settled the question. "I have never had *kouskous*," she says aloud.

"It's seldom served in this country. It's an Arabian food which is prepared of vegetables, meats, almonds, and with a variety of herbs and spices. I assure you, it is an extremely appetizing mixture."

Akin leans back and watches von Riefenbach strike a new chord which begins the farandole dance for the third time. Isn't it strange, she says to herself, how a musician knows what music can be played twice, three times in succession, without losing its interest? It is a custom with her, also, to repeat a piece, a piece that is lovely, over and over.

As the dance is played, Akin reflects upon the life she will have with von Riefenbach.

The day the child is born, I will give it to him, she thinks to herself. "This is *our* child,"

I will say to him as he stands over my bed looking at the infant lying next to me. "It is yours and mine, dear Ludwig."

"It is *yours,* more than mine," he will say with tears flooding his eyes. He will appear saintly at that moment, and a brilliant light will glow above his head. He will take my hand and say, "Although I am not the father, my darling Akin, I shall love the child as though he were my own."

"I know," I'll say, turning to the child, "you are the father, Ludwig. Look . . . he even resembles you a bit."

And he'll smile, as he comes nearer—almost afraid to breathe heavily on the new born child. "And that, too, will be enough," he'll say, touching the child's small hand. "Even the accident that he should bear my features." He'll wait a moment, then he'll say, "But he resembles you, my darling. The same almond eyes, the same beautiful chin. It's a beautiful baby, Akin."

The child will begin crying and Ludwig will want to take it up in his arms to rock it gently. But I will gently prevent him. "It is your child also," I'll say. "It is your child as well as mine. You are the father, Ludwig." He will not understand what I mean. "The father of the child is he who is there when it is born, he who is ready to take it up in his arms and to comfort it, he who walks the child and gives it his love." He will look at me from beside the bed. The child in my arms will be lying quietly. And Ludwig will smile. "The father is not the one who has enjoyed the reverie of love but who doesn't pay for it," I'll say almost in a whisper. "You are the father, Ludwig. The child is yours."

And in time, thinks Akin as she takes another cigarette and lights it, I will have grown old. I will be able to look back at my youth and know —know that I have not missed those things which I have longed for.

"What ever became of Alex?" my brother Ezra will say to me one day years after the child has grown up and is away at school. "Have you ever heard from him again?" he'll ask in his old manner of being wise, of knowing.

"No, Ezra. I have never heard from Alex," I'll say. I'll remember the stories which Peter told me through the years, stories about Alex. "I had a feeling from the start that Alex was possessed."

"Now, dear sister, don't be abstract. What do you mean, 'possessed'?" He'll continue. "What you mean is, he was a tramp right from the beginning."

"I don't mean that at all, Ezra. I know that is what you've always thought about him. But with Alex it was another story entirely." I'll find myself loyally defending Alex, and remembering the way he looked in those earlier days. "No, Ezra," I will say, "I learned there was something deeper in him, even before he went away—something which had control of his reasoning. And then, after he was gone, I knew how it went with him from his letters—first to me and later to Peter—how he began by befriending all kinds of morbid and perverse people; how when he reached Africa, he went about dressed as a sage of the old, old times; and how, finally, in Egypt, his mind began to crack completely from our lives. In one of his last letters to me

he told of his compulsion to fling himself at
the feet of one of those great statues which
guard the gates of some temple half-lost in the
sands." Ezra will look at me his most wither-
ingly, but I will go on. "Yes, Ezra. Later he
went to the Black Sea, compelled from within."

"In other words, he was bats, wouldn't you
say? And isn't that about the time he was writing to you about destroying the child?" Ezra
will say, although he will be somewhat fascinated by the uncertainty, the mystery, of what
became of Alex. He will wish that he had followed the story before this.

"Yes, it was then," I'll say. And I'll create a
story for Ezra, as I created a story for Alex
years ago.

"When Alex returned to Cairo from the
Upper Nile, he felt that he had learned the answer he was seeking, the meaning of his life.
He wrote to me once that he was writing a
Journal which would earn him money to send
for me. But that was only another of the fan-
tasies which hovered about his destiny. When
he arrived at Alexandria, he learned about the
child and wrote telling me that it would be

impossible for us to have it—'until we are worthy of the divine gift of creation,' he had said."

"You see?" Ezra will cut in again, "he was mad. Tell me, dear sister, what happened afterwards?"

"Some days after I had received his letter, I realized that Alex didn't love me at all. I hadn't known, before, what it was that was driving him further and further away from me. Alex never loved me, you see. He had built an illusion of what I should have been, and he worshipped the illusion." I'll then remember the last letter I wrote to him. "I wrote Alex a last letter that day, telling him that we were through."

"But what happened to him afterwards?" Ezra will persist. His voice will sound like Alex's just then: the same voice Alex used when he had insisted that I continue with the story about the ode. "You say that he went on to the Black Sea?"

"Yes, he went on at least to Constantinople. And there he received my last letter. He didn't seem to take my letter seriously, however, for he wrote to me many times thereafter, as though everything were the same between us. I never answered the letters, though. I returned them, unopened."

"Did he ever get the money to send for you."

"I don't know," I'll say, wondering to myself whether he really did. "Meanwhile, I had met Ludwig. I fell in love with him and knew that my relationship with Alex was only a childish dream."

"And that was the end of it, I suppose," Ezra will say, and thinking that he was not totally mistaken about Alex, after all.

"It was the end of it so far as I was concerned. Yes, that was the end." But I'll want to impress Ezra with knowing also what became of Alex, and so I'll say, "From Constantinople Alex went further East. I don't know exactly where— India, I believe, or Ceylon. . . . I was told that while he was in India he took on a friend, a young Swiss count whom he had met briefly long before in France. The young count, still in his 'teens, became fascinated by Alex's strange life. He became devoted to him. They lived together, wandering about the world for a few years, and then the Swiss boy died." Yes, the story is coming to an end, I'll think to myself. "It was strange, this relationship with the count, Ezra, for Alex had begun to read the Tarot cards—or some such mystical thing—and he predicted his friend's death quite some time before it happened, after which it was an unfortunate life they led together. Alex took to drugs —first kief, then hashish, finally cocaine. And the count died without Alex even aware of his loss. . . . As I have heard the story, he was taken in at one of the missions one day and the monks gave him odd jobs for his keep. Since then, none of us has heard of him."

Ezra will have been delighted by the story. He'll look at me and say, "I bet he had always been frustrated. He probably wanted a son, though probably not a real one of his own, but an illusion. That's why he went mad. That's why he wouldn't accept the fact of a real son, when you told him about your child. That's why he took on the Swiss boy and finally went insane entirely. He should have gone to see a psychiatrist," Ezra will conclude sedately.

"That may have been it," I'll say. Ezra's conclusion will be valid, too, as was Alex's to my first story. "He was possessed, you see," I'll say.

"I'll be right back," says von Riefenbach, turning and smiling. He has finished the dance and is walking across the room. "I want to make certain the cook prepares dinner for two."

Just as he starts to go through the beaded door, Akin calls out to him, "Where is the telephone?"

"Just there, behind you, in the corner next to the drape."

"Thank you," says she, walking to the telephone. She dials her brother's number. His phone rings one, twice, three times—but there is no reply. Akin holds the receiver a moment longer. He must be out, says she to herself and returns to the sofa. I wonder where he could be?

As she leans back in the chair, blood rushes to her head. An agonizing pain comes to her stomach. She bends over, head almost touching her knees, and begins blacking out.

What is happening? She hears a voice speak

to her above the pain. Why am I here? What have I been thinking about?

The pain grows stronger. I'll take you out of this place, says Akin to the inner voice. She rises to her feet and her cigarette falls to the floor.

She walks to the archway, looks back at the room, sees her pencil box on the small table.— Go after the purse, the inner voice says to her. And she returns for it.—I have it, says Akin above the pain, and walks down the first hall- way, left down the second, then down out of the building.

೭§ 4. THE MORNING OF THE HATHOR

Characters

Reuben   *a cab driver*

Others

Mrs. Waldbom   *landlady*

The Morning of the Hathor

At the first corner, a taxi pulls to the curb on the wrong side of the street. It stops a few feet from Akin.

"Hey!" a voice calls out to her from the taxi. "Where you goin', kid?"

Akin is still dazed, her stomach is still aching. Someone is calling you, says the inner voice. She walks over to the taxi, bends down slightly, and recognizes the driver's face. Akin continues starting at him while her thoughts clear.

"Get in, kid," says the driver, wondering what is wrong with her.

Akin gets on the back seat and the taxi drives away.

It is late and the street lights have been on for an hour. The taxi turns north on Broadway,

and the driver pulls down the plate glass behind his head.

"What are you doin' around here?" says he
in a loud voice. He is an old friend of Akin's,
and he is hard of hearing. "I thought you was
living across the river these days?"

"I was visiting a friend," she replies, barely
able to lift her voice. Things begin to seem
somewhat normal to her now, and the pain begins to leave. She leans toward the open plate-
glass window and says, "I'm hungry, Reuben."

"Wha'd you say?" says he, slowing down the
taxi and pulling over to the curb. "Wha'd you
say?" The taxi stops.

"I'm hungry," says Akin, louder. "I haven't
eaten all day!" she shouts at the top of her
voice.

"You haven't eaten? Is that what you said,
kid?" says Reuben, turning off the ignition.
"Come up front. . . . I can't hear you."

Akin gets on the front seat next to Reuben
and places her pencil box between them. She
isn't certain whether it's a good thing or not
that Reuben is there with her at this moment.

Akin has known him for a long time. She met

him back when she was living with her brother on 56th Street—in fact it was the same evening that Alex came to say goodbye before his trip to Arizona. She was lonely that night. She walked all the way to Harlem without money in her purse. And it was Reuben who gave her a lift back.

She had seen him several times afterwards, and when Alex left for Bordeaux, she had seen him again.

"Wha'd you say over there?" shouts Reuben for the third time. His face is unshaven and he is wearing an old, black-leather jacket. His eyes are child-like, and his husky body seems cramped behind the wheel. On his collar he wears a small badge with numbers printed under a miniature photograph of himself. The third finger of his right hand is missing.

"I'm very, very hungry," shouts Akin in return, and dramatizing a forlorn expression so that he will not misunderstand.

"You're hungry, eh kid? I'll fix that." Reuben starts the motor once more and continues driving up Broadway. We'll go over to my joint," says he leaning his head toward Akin. "There's sure to be stuff in the ice-box."

"That's lovely, Reuben," says Akin, deciding that it was because of this, because she was hungry, that she had gotten a cramp in her stomach up in von Riefenbach's apartment.

"Wha'd you say?" shouts Reuben.

"Nothing much," Akin shouts back. "I was only saying that it looks like the rain is never going to let up."

Reuben turns up the speed of the windshield wiper.

Reuben's room is on West Eighty-Fourth Street—a room and a bath, straight to the rear of the building, on the main floor.

Akin and Reuben enter quietly. She quickly walks over to the ice-box, takes a slice of salami, then goes to the large double bed and lies down. She is too exhausted to prepare the food. She lets her shoes drop to the floor.

"Reuben!" shouts Akin to the taxi-driver, who has gone into the bathroom.

"Wha'd you say?" says he coming back into the bedroom and still buttoning the fly of his trousers. He has taken off his jacket and is in his shirt sleeves.

"You're sick, eh kid?" says he, not clearly hearing her words but guessing what she has said.

"Yes, I'm sick," says Akin. She turns on her side and faces the blank wall. Reuben turns off the lamp and gets into bed beside her.

"We'll eat later," says he, and pulls her back around. Akin doesn't resist him. She has known Reuben this way before. But she edges her knees up close to her waist.

"I'm very tired," says she in his ear. The taxi-driver unbuttons Akin's blouse and he caresses her bare ankles.

"You're hungry, eh kid?" says he finally, and pulls off his trousers.

"Okay, kid," says Reuben getting up, turning on the light switch at the door, and going over to the shelves above the ice-box. He takes down two dishes. "You stay there and take it easy. I'll handle the food." He prepares salami sandwiches and puts a pot of water on the gas stove. "You can take your choice," says he. "Milk or coffee?"

Akin doesn't reply. She has covered her head with a pillow to shield her eyes from the glare of the naked bulb just above her head. "You'd better have milk, if you're feelin' sick."

Reuben brings the two dishes and places them on the small night-table near the bed. Akin raises herself a bit, takes one of the sandwiches and the glass of milk.

"Wha's the matter with you, kid?" says he in a low voice as he pours himself coffee.

"I'm going to have a baby," says Akin with her mouth holding food. She looks at her stomach and then back at Reuben, who is standing now with a stupified expression on his face.

"Wha'd you say? What's the matter with you, kid? Are you pregnant?" He is still holding the pot and comes nearer the bed. "It looks like you're gonna have a baby," says he kneeling and pressing his nose almost to Akin's stomach.

"Yes, it looks that way, doesn't it?" she says, half laughing to herself.

"Who's the father?" says Reuben, drawing back and taking a bite from his sandwich.

"God only knows," says Akin, blinking her eyes and realizing for the first time that it's possible Alex is not the father. But how could that be? she questions herself. Of course it's Alex's. —It couldn't be . . . anyone else's.

Reuben drives Akin to the station early the following morning. He buys her a ticket to Roselle, gives her the remaining small change from his pocket, and waits with her until the train departs.

Once on the train, Akin takes the letter she has written to Alex out of her pencil box and tears it into small pieces. Why send him the letter anyway? she thinks to herself. Why bother now?

Akin is happy that she is returning to her small room in Roselle, happy to get away from the city. Yesterday has been too long a day, too strenuous, she says to herself.

As the train rushes through the tunnel, Akin stares at herself in the window beside her. How silly I was, says she to herself, for having gotten angry yesterday morning. There was no need for losing my temper, writing that letter, dashing off to Manhattan. . . . And for what? To see Ezra? Peter? To meet von Riefenbach? What nonsense. I should know better than that, Akin says out loud to her own image in the window. I should have known better than to lose my temper.

Light splashes away Akin's face in the window. The train is now passing through the dull, New Jersey landscape. And besides, continues Akin, as she sits stately and dignified with her eyes half closed and her chin raised high, I'm a woman now.

"There's a letter for you at the house, dearie," says a voice as Akin is walking slowly out the station gate. She looks up. It's her landlady.

"What did you say, Mrs. Waldbom?"

"I say there's a letter for you at the house." The heavy-set woman begins walking along with Akin. "It's been there since yesterday noon, dearie," says she.

"I'm sorry I wasn't at the house yesterday, Mrs. Waldbom," says Akin, trying not to appear anxious about the letter. "I left for the

city early. I spent all day with my brother
Ezra."

"Oh that's all right, dearie. You know I
don't mind when you don't come in," says her
landlady. "I only thought you might like to
know there's mail for you. I left it under your
door." Mrs. Waldbom stops. "I've got to go
back to the station now. My train leaves any
minute and my husband will kill me if I don't
go across to Brooklyn today to see his mother.
She's sick, you know, dearie. Poor thing." She
takes Akin's hand a moment, then says, "Be a
good girl, dearie, and I'll see you when I get
back this evening. Bye, bye, dearie," says she
and goes off in the direction of the station.

Akin walks quickly. Each block to the rooming house seems endless to her now. A car, coming on full speed, honks its horn at her. Honk!
Honk! Akin pays no attention and walks on as
though nothing else in the world mattered but
the letter waiting for her under her door. It begins raining lightly.

I've wasted an entire day, says Akin to herself as she begins walking faster. I should never
have left the house yesterday. I'm so foolish, she

scolds herself as her steps switch into a trot. I'm so foolish, she repeats. I'm so foolish.

At Eighth Street Akin slows up. She is exhausted and breathing deeply. But when she arrives at her rooming house, she mounts the stairs to her room on the run. She unlocks the door and throws it open.

Akin picks up the letter on the floor at her feet. Her fingers are trembling as she tears open the envelope without noting where it's from.

Akin darling:

I've just redone the apartment—lavender, beige and chartreuse—and I'm giving a cocktail party Friday. Be sure to be here: at 4 p.m. sharp. There will be some special friends I want you to meet (in particular a wealthy 'cellist named Ludwig von Riefenbach, son of R. G. von Riefenbach).

Your loving brother,
Ezra

Akin walks to the center of the room as she crumples the note in her hand. Tears flood her almond-shaped eyes, and the rain begins pouring down heavily outside the open window. Akin walks over to the window, throws the note out, turns around, and faces the dark wall.

A hazel-colored Hathor, miniature size, stands on the circular table. The table and an ironpost bed are the furnishings of the rented room in Roselle, New Jersey. And the Hathor is a statue—*the Goddess of Social Joy*—sent to Akin Arahk from the upper Nile by Alex L——, who is now somewhere on the Black Sea. Akin walks to the table, takes the Hathor and holds it for a moment; then she smashes it on the tiled floor below the wash basin. She is angry with Alex for having left her behind.

Akin is going to sit for an hour at the open window, playing an oboe. She sits stiffly, with her chin raised high. Her slender fingers hold the instrument with delicate patronage, while the fragile, reed mouthpiece is brought forward, upward, and is held in mid-air. Her head remains fixed as her eyes search the floor at her feet, where lay two fragments of the broken Hathor.